A Chaos of Light

NEW WRITING SCOTLAND 43

Edited by
Kirstin Innes
and
Chris Powici

Gaelic editor:
Niall O'Gallagher

Association for Scottish Literature

Association for Scottish Literature
Scottish Literature, 7 University Gardens
University of Glasgow, Glasgow G12 8QH
www.asls.org.uk

ASL is a registered charity no. SC006535

First published 2025
© Association for Scottish Literature
and the individual contributors

This is a work of human endeavour. No large-language models
or text-to-image generators ('generative AI') were used
in the creation or production of this book.

British Library Cataloguing in Publication Data
A CIP record for this book is available
from the British Library

ISBN 978-1-906841-66-9

Our authorised representative in the EU for product safety is
JGU Scotland HUB, Johannes Gutenberg Universität Mainz
Jakob-Welder-Weg 18, 55128 Mainz, Germany
scotland@uni-mainz.de

The Association for Scottish Literature
acknowledges the support of Creative Scotland
towards the publication of this book

Typeset in Minion Pro and Sofia Pro Soft by ASL
Printed by Ashford Colour Ltd, Gosport

CONTENTS

Introduction v
New Writing Scotland 44: submission instructions vii

Craig Aitchison	First / Babel / Murmur / Last	1
Sharon Black	Christmas Drinks	5
Niki Brennan	Croft / You have a pot of stew cooking / Rabbit Season	7
Kevin Cormack	Shoracks / Guts	13
Mila Daskalova	The Holiday	16
Rodge Glass	Return to 'The Gorbals'	24
Reyzl Grace	Brigadoon / The Witchin Oor	34
Lydia Harris	Mary Dykes Brown / Request to Fife Bereavement Services / Words to conjure strong protections for White Moss / the key is that Mary died . .	39
Stella Hervey Birrell	Your back reminds me of Christ of Saint John of the Cross / Christmas Eve Sonnet, 2022 / Lost Property . .	44
Elizabeth Ingram Wallace . .	Thick Lines of Sky and Scissor Sharp Suns	47
Karen Jones	Straw Woman	53
Allie Kerper	Sext After Therapy / ASMR Girlfriend Mutual Attention Vignettes Stream of Consciousness (Softspoken, Relaxing)	57
Marcas Mac an Tuairneir . .	Eithne / Coille Ghallaibh / Mac-meanmna / An Caolas	59
Donnchadh MacCàba	Às Ùr / Sgòthan	67
Crìsdean MacIlleBhàin . . .	Ainglean	70
Scott McNee	Up Beinn Chabhair	82
Kevin MacNeil	Morning is Broken	89
Kathleen J. Marshall	The Sum of His Misfortunes	99

Philip Miller	On Being Poisoned	104
Victoria Nic̀lomlair	Deireadh Shamhraidh / Gach Oidhche	109
Audrey Niven	My heart is a super-bounce ball	111
Amy Jo Philip	14.6	112
Petra Johana Poncarová	Cumha	115
Julie Rea	Ashes to Ashes	118
Zain Rishi	Pillars / Skunks in the Mall	126
Romi Sarfaty	not so hard to imagine	129
Neil Gordon Shaw	19 September 2014	140
Joey Simons	Sant Eulalia	143
Zusana Storrier	Renovations	146
Kirsty Strang-Roy	Persephone	148
Laura Tansley	Once a man said to me fuck you David Cameron	150
Tim Turnbull	Gerald Ford	152
Emily Utter	Slivers	154
Laura Walker	Inch	158
Lynnda Wardle	Visiting Cairnbaan	163
Christie Williamson	At Inverboyndie	164
Robin Lindsay Wilson	Risk Avoidance	165

Author biographies 167

INTRODUCTION

New Writing Scotland has a wide-open editorial policy, and we read each submission anonymously. It can create a lot of reading for our three-strong editorial team (two reading English and Scots, one Gaelic), but that policy pays dividends when it comes to pulling together a properly broad portrait of Scottish writing right now.

You might find few thematic similarities between the entries in the pages of this book, but you'll find scope, range and diversity. Writers young and old, living in and outwith Scotland, across a broad stretch of cultural traditions and styles.

What particularly struck us this year was writers striving to push Scots writing beyond the still all-too-potent tropes of the kailyard or the Glasgow hard man. Kevin Cormack shunts Orcadian-infused Scots into angry, rhythmic reminiscence; Reyzl Grace re-configures the Brigadoon myth to show with compelling lyricism how modern Scots gives voice to the energies of desire. The intimate entanglement of history, geography and identity inform the cadences and vocabulary of Amy Jo Philip's '14.6' (as does a well-honed relish for a good single malt). In these pages Scots has been used with an open heart and an open mind, a well-tuned alertness to modernity as well as tradition.

There is, of course, also some phenomenal writing in English and Gaelic – writing of wit, intelligence, skill, imagination and courage. The disarmingly charming exploration of friendship in Kevin MacNeil's 'Morning is Broken' isn't so much thought-provoking as thought-inviting. Maybe it's more important to learn how to mend things (and people) well than hope they don't break in the first place. In 'Renovations', Zusana Storrier raises intriguing questions about who owns the past, and who visits and who lives there, and you'd be hard put to find a more sinuously graceful poem about love and home, hurt and beauty, than Zain Rishi's 'Pillars'.

But these are not stories and poems that serve up easy answers and trite explanations. The spirit of that wide-open call out –

come-all-ye – burns brightly in writing that unsettles and challenges, that questions assumptions and gets us to look *at*, when it feels so much less painful to look *away*. The shadow of conflict in Palestine falls so starkly and movingly over Rodge Glass's 'Return to "The Gorbals"' and Romi Sarfaty's 'not so hard to imagine' because the writers don't stake out their claim to truth in the barren soil of polemics; instead, they tell uncomfortable, troubling human stories. In other words, this is, above all, *good* writing. Elsewhere, Audrey Niven evokes with beguiling poignancy the awful proximity of playground and battleground for those living in Faslane's potential fall-out zone in 'My heart is a super-bounce ball'.

The pressing truth of just how hard it is to be out of work and broke, or even *in* work and broke, reverberates throughout *New Writing Scotland* 43, including the description of a 'zero hours counter, a gig-economy first responder' in Robin Lindsay Wilson's 'Risk Avoidance'. That poverty is a cultural as well as an economic malaise is explored to telling effect by Tim Turnbull in 'Gerald Ford'. In times as strange as these, who's to say a fibreglass president isn't preferable to the real thing?

There is also a seam of work here – as exemplified by Kirsty Strang-Roy's visceral nature-fiction 'Persephone', the piece from which we've borrowed this year's title – that steps away from the turbulent churn of the zeitgeist to just breathe, look around, engage with myth or nature, or both.

So here you go. A rich, boisterous, tender, charming, angry, sorrowful, gleeful mix of writing. Different ways of living in and questioning the world rub shoulders; and if occasionally, you feel moved to disagree (or raise your voice in praise) – well, good. That's as it should be. In poems, short stories, novel extracts, scripts and memoir, the writers featured in these pages have found their own distinctive ways of giving voice to what matters to them, and thereby spill some of the familiar, surprising, awkward, thrilling truths that make up who we are.

Kirstin Innes and Chris Powici

NEW WRITING SCOTLAND 44: SUBMISSION INSTRUCTIONS

The forty-fourth volume of *New Writing Scotland* will be published in summer 2026. Submissions are invited from writers resident in Scotland or Scots by birth, upbringing or inclination. All forms of writing are welcome: autobiography and memoirs; creative responses to events and experiences; drama; graphic artwork (monochrome only, of suitable size); poetry; political and cultural commentary and satire; short fiction; travel writing or any other creative prose may be submitted, but not full-length plays or novels, though self-contained extracts are acceptable. The work must be entirely your own and produced without the assistance of generative AI. It must not be previously published or accepted for publication elsewhere, and may be written in any of the languages of Scotland. Submissions should be uploaded, for free, via Submittable:

nws.submittable.com/submit

Prose pieces should be double-spaced and carry an approximate word-count. Please do not put your name on your submission; instead, please provide your name and contact details, including email and postal addresses, on a covering letter. If you are sending more than one piece, please group everything into one document. **Please send no more than four poems, or one prose work.**

Authors retain all rights to their work(s) and are free to submit and/or publish the same work(s) elsewhere after they appear in *New Writing Scotland*. Successful contributors will be paid at a rate of £50 for the first published page and £25 for each subsequent published page.

Please be aware that we have limited space in each edition, and therefore shorter pieces are more suitable – although longer items of exceptional quality may still be included. Our maximum suggested word-count is 3,500 words, and the submission deadline is midnight on **31 October 2025.**

Craig Aitchison
FIRST

'How did language start? Why?'
—Sam NicFhionghain, age 9

Mibbe leid echas bow-wow an mew, chirl
an chitter, plash o burns, chirp o bird,
howl o beasties. Dis that straik an inner
chord, mak kist an whame, banes an blood piver?

Or ding-dong, la-la, yo-he-ho, pooh-pooh?
Single seed plantit in rich sile, ready
tae grow. Genetic mutation, an unco
airt tae build an biggen, the stoot an steidy

seekin. Sae mony attempts tae locate
the soorce – frontal cortex, Broca's area,
some shaw or den in ancient Africa,
where humans, while gruimin, fund a new wey

tae connect, lowse what wis locked in their ain sel,
tae speak a pyne, tae shape a caw for help.

BABEL

First, a still, a stound in the lee.
Seelence faws. Awbody, awthin
stops. A glisk, een meet, folk see
a sharet fear, a mutual kennin.
A blink. A leam that blints. Then mirk.
The air bevvers, tremmles, fissles;
folk wake frae their dwaum, skirt awey,
but fear follaes, nips and birsles.
A gowst, a bleddum an blatter.
Bang. A stramash. The grand tooer
crummles, words skirl an scaiter,
soond turns tae smusht mirk stoor.
Folk in aw airts cairry the merk
faint as a hishie in the derk.

MURMUR

Tae begin wi, nithin. A page withoot
pictur, merk. Then what seems juist a screeble
withoot airt. But they haunds sae carefu,
linkin a wey through snaw-white, findin a route

somewhere. Ilka step nearhaund the same –
line, twae loops. *Hanzi?* Some oorie word
scrieved ower and ower, some need tae rhame,
let flee some quate, dern kennin. Wings! Birds!

Birds flichter intae life. Gaitherin flock
on the page. A fleein murmuration
lifts, birls, turns itsel inside oot, swellin
an joukin, coordinatit by sic

focus an flow, a synchronised thrang
that speaks in yin bonnie, urgent sang.

LAST

The last tae ken aw the words for rain –
*rain that briskens or drooks, rain sair needit,
no wantit.* Wi cootlin, coaxin she blethert,
sic words, sae mony tae be lost sae sin.

A listen, ettlin tae gresp meanins, scrieve
jottins, sclent, nearhaund attempts tae captur
a resemmlance, a shade even, afore
they're loast. *Kennin it's impossible, tae strive;*

Dreams that stey efter wakin, yon word near
*rootit, nourishin, nourisht; belongin
tae land an folk; licht reflectin
aff rinnin water.* Mair, sae much mair.

But withoot the souch o her vyce, they're juist
waesome exiles, stravaigers, lanely, lost.

Sharon Black
CHRISTMAS DRINKS

Like any other evening, really: the spill
into the bar, first glass then the rest,

making of the blood a sweet mystery,
Janice from the subs desk

passing round her Corfu snaps,
Alanis's *You Oughta Know*, me sliding

underneath the table to the barman,
his hand a tulip, tender, white,

him letting go, my body a fruit machine
on a winning streak – *ching, ching, ching* –

three oranges, three watermelons –
someone stepping on a chair, the table,

that someone being me –
a helium balloon, a sequin, a golden cut-out

at the summit of the tree – the manager
called, my boss swimming

into focus at the door, hand across my back –
Christmas bonus, Young Feature Writer of the Year

dancing in the street, the taxi
refusing to take me, Sue trying to

put me in her car, me running away, police,
cuffs, cell, fired next day – words

like 'reputation', 'character', 'respect'.
It was years till I could let her be – swaying

down Ingram Street to George Square
in rhinestone boots to *Common People*,

sidling up to Walter Scott, chucking him
from his eighty-foot-high Doric column, climbing up,

off my face, the whole of Glasgow at my feet,
a glittering '90s monument to myself.

Niki Brennan
CROFT

In the town he dies in, rainfall is not measured
in millimetres, but in skin – in its reminder

of things to be mended: a failure of the wool
or the cobbling, thatching that beacons the season.

In the fields, the crop farmer's son leans against his scythe,
his hands on the small of its back – they could be dancing;

the biting waltz of wood, slick from open blisters,
a misplaced slice through the stubborn forehead of a turnip.

By night, he washes his sores in the river,
the curving fronds of time misspent

lean heavy on his shoulders, he questions the rain:
how water fills everything, and nothing.

By morning, he worships in the crofter's cottage.
He studies the stones like books,

mouthing the names of his fathers; the labyrinth
of their fingerprints, their signatures on the underside

like woodlice – he knows them by shape and sound,
this quiet pride, this indulgence; he wishes he could

place them on his tongue and feel them dissolve into him.
He can't explain this feeling

but when he steps outside to feed the dogs
and loosen their chains,

he wants to stoop in the mud with them,
to never tire barking at clouds.

YOU HAVE A POT OF STEW COOKING

and I haven't heard my name said the hard way in a while.

Its edges buttered over distance and time, its pointed ends
patted into rounds, its sharpness sweet in other throats.

I'm beginning to belong to something that isn't quite mine
like the salt in the soil underneath my fingernails, breaking

to return to a body that knows it through.
But here, in a kitchen where I know which things need

to be closed twice; where not to step at four a.m.;
my skin is softer here. I am slow in wanting.

Because I know you're like me – you want
to put your lips to something that has only ever felt teeth.

And I wonder with my mouth full of something dead
but warm, something that aches of home,

how you screwed the bolts, attached the clamps,
summoned the lightning, beckoned my howl –

how love, for us, is always in a state
of return, of gathering the pieces

and burying the remains and praying
for what doesn't. You sat where I sit,

wiping your mouth on the back of your hand,
questioning who you were with the same dirt on your knees

from reasoning with the end, from soaking
a slice of bread in the gravy and feeding the earth.

RABBIT SEASON

    the night dressed up as forever
        in the passenger seat of your car
            just dash and a curd of moon,
            radio hand signals
        your knucklebones ancient, throttling the wheel
    hitting eighty or something into nothing

    even lavender is black in winter nights, even thistles are soft
           against the velvet,
        even your lips, a smile

    the name a greeting, the car the outstretched hand
           mine grasping at rhubarb and custards,
        sweating in plastic

on my knees to peer, even then I knew
    it was a position of piety
        or of begging

        the corridors of light, the long road sickening
            they were running, faster than anything
        anything, really, I swear

then the tender
    bump
the empty road ahead, smooth as your jawbone

I had seen it all before, of course
        men with spears on the walls of caves in the pages of books
    and men with guns in television shows
        where nothing survived

And then my scream
    the delight of new discovery. The raspberry sauce
        at the bottom of the wafer cone.
            An echo in the dead of night, sounding out ahead.
    An accomplice to an end.
    For barely even a mouthful of meat.

Kevin Cormack
SHORACKS

fur Tony Swain

This wis whin TVs hid thir oun national bedtime:
a vicar in a comfortable, high-backed chair
wid shepherd his mild-mannered story
aboot a window cleaner, or a trip tae the seaside,
twaards hids inevitable punchline:
'And, you know, Jesus was a bit like that.'
At these words the TV wid sink intae a sea o white noise.
We convened in her mither's attic,
oan an owld couch beneath the cooples,
and stared at yin churnan blizzard fur oors oan end.
Hunkered in front o her mither's muted Grundig,
a year since wir last meeteen, we drifted oot again
intae a dwam until figures appeared.
The hoose below breathed like bellows
o an accordion; a timorous whistle, me squeaky eyes.
The attic lowed like a crystal haal, last I saa her –
dark-eyed and ready tae furgit me.
I wid lean intae that storm (o some demiurge's
makeen) the rest o me days.
Sheu leant in different – like bliindie-bockie –
and disappeared intae tambourines and mirrors.

Shoracks: *shore-dwellers of Kirkwall*
bliindie-bockie: *blind man's buff*

GUTS
i.m. K. H.

'You know more than I know' sang John Cale,
under the needle in yir student digs, twinned
wae mine. Words afore I worded thum;
clippeens o feteesh and crime scenes
afore the inkleen, the glue, the compositional eye.
Whar ye came fae and whar ye then dwelt:
that fraction o a second afore sense
reaches the brain, raffles up wae emotion,
laughter lippers ower. Whar stimuli bides
in the raa, afore adoption: colourless colour,
touchless touch and ither such blethers.

Makan me whit? A cover version – a bad wan
at that – wae virry little say in the metter?
Me intimidatan mate, as mates so often err.
The Mekon in Bowie's black leather jaiket
fae the cover o *Heroes*, riflan through
vintage paperback emporiums,
as if elbuck-deep in a buullick's liver.
Lendan me biographies o resplendent,
reckless lives – hand-me-doon
subversion fur yir second-hand sael –
designed tae mak me less and less sure.

Fae somebuddy thit nivver bowt a stick
o furnityir in his life, nivver ouwned
a fridge or washeen machine, hoose or ker,
computer or smertphone.
Zeus (as played bae Niall MacGinnis)
geen foosty in a ruined picture-hoose attic.

That's the *trouble wae classicists*:
liable tae spang clear o the membrane entirely.
Blessed be the latecomers – the gulf
between stoory needle crackle
and yir bureaucratic bowels.

Mila Daskalova
THE HOLIDAY

Marin is the god of this place. He marches along the shore in his red shorts, just-as-red cap, and yellow t-shirt bearing his divine title, 'Lifeguard'. His sunglasses hide his eyes, giving him a stern, steely look. His big belly is deceptive. While on land he moves with slow, wobbly machismo, in water he transforms into a swift, graceful walrus. Once a day, and once a day only, when the sun is at its highest point, Marin sheds his t-shirt, puts his sunglasses on his chair and glides into the salty waters. His arms move fast, mechanically, one stroke following the other without fatigue or doubt. He is the god and we, the lazy, foolish tourists who have been washed off on his shore from all corners of the world like seaweed, are his subjects, his lost sheep.

He spends his day resting on his foldable chair under the shade of the parasol, only raising himself to collect taxes from newcomers. While seated, he is always staring at the sea, so it's a mystery how he sees them. Another proof of His omniscience. He is tanned but unburned, unlike the rest of us mortals.

Today I reach the beach at 7:30 a.m., coming straight from my bed. There is no one else, apart from Marin and Ivan, and they have not yet taken their usual positions: Marin on his foldable throne and Ivan behind the bar. Marin is preparing for the day, rebuilding the beach world he dismantled the previous night – dragging lounge chairs across the dusty sand, throwing cushions on them, spreading the parasols, emptying ash trays. I find Ivan breaking his fast with a pile of hard-boiled eggs and a bowl of rice. I apologise for interrupting his meal and ask for a coffee.

Ivan is the type of man that intimidates and amuses me all at once. He is god's substitute here. His t-shirt is red. His eyes are also hidden – closed, open, or missing altogether. He is a triangular mass of hard, awe-inspiring flesh. I have never seen him go near the water.

'Short or long?' he grunts benevolently, granting me the choice between a less or more watery espresso.

'Long, please!'

A longer espresso cools down more slowly, giving me time to have a quick swim before I have my first sip.

At this time of day, the black sea is still asleep. I bathe my own sleepy restlessness in it, that feeling sleepwalkers must feel when they rise from their beds in their blind search of dreams. I lie down, floating, eyes closed. The water is cool like silk, yet untainted by the sunscreen of anointed worshippers who will join me later. I am alone, but I know I am observed from behind black glasses.

Only underwater can I hide from the unblinking, all-seeing eyes. I take a deep breath and dive. The water is murky. Little pieces of seaweed swirl among a mass of sandy glitter. The opaqueness comforts me. If I can't see, I can't be seen.

But my privacy is temporary. I have to go back up, once the lungs shrink and crease. My legs will soon start kicking, and I will reappear, maybe a few metres away from the place of submersion but always on the same beach. My privacy is conditional too. I know that if I will my legs to stillness and refuse to reappear, I will have to face Marin's omnipresence too. The walrus-god will find me in the opaque sea water and singlehandedly exile me from my hidden heaven. I wonder how long I can hold my breath, my freedom. What are the limits of His patience?

I decide not to test it. I go up, swim back. Misjudging the depth, I reach out my foot to find the sea floor and discover it with my knee. I stumble out of the sea and fall on my lounge chair, belly up, breathless like a fish.

The coffee is just right. I sip it, taking cover in my towel. More people crawl on the dusty road down the hill. The sun is gentle still, preparing to scorch us all. No wind. I lie down and try to rest my mind. The sound of waves and bare feet rearranging seashell dust. I forget time and the distance I have traversed to be here. I stray away from images of other places I want to be at, of eyes

I wish were here to witness me becoming pure breath. Light and lightness. I am astonished to discover I can still be happily out of place, unplaceable.

A few hours pass fast in perfect stillness, like the ground observed from a plane high up in the clouds. As I dry stretched out under the morning sun, Marin's voice booms suddenly, startling seagulls, sunbathers, and thoughts:

'How many times do I have to repeat?!'

He has said nothing all day. His voice is like coarse sea salt. He is standing, with his hands on his hips and his feet in the water, ready to morph into his sea-form.

'Come back here, or I'll push your head underwater, to see how you like it!'

All eyes move away from him to the fool who has disobeyed His will. Close to the alarming red dot of the final buoy, we see a white cap hovering over the folds of a pink neck. Beyond that – the waves of a sea in a frenzy, fully awake, suicidally galloping and crashing into the side of the bay. Without a hurry, the white hat turns 180 degrees and begins to move towards us at the pace of a lazy breaststroke.

'Idiots,' the disgruntled god mumbles under his nose, loud enough for all of us, the obedient ones, to hear.

I close my eyes and wish quick and immediate death upon the White Cap who has tested His patience and ruined our collective peace.

Two o'clock. I pretend to read, while spying on my neighbours. A pastime with a long-standing tradition here in Bulgaria. It can be practiced both by amateurs, such as nosy old ladies peeking out from their balconies, and professionals with eyes shaped like keyholes.

The woman of the umbrella to my left is getting a massage. Her husband (or man friend, or secret lover) is holding a phone raised in front of his chest, capturing the process. Maybe later they will watch it together, laughing at the masseur, Marin's loyal half-naked priest garbed in the red shorts characteristic of this summer religion and a massive chain with a heavy-looking cross – a relic of the religion practiced during the rest of the year. Or maybe the husband will view the video in solitude months later, when the holiday is over and autumn trench coats hide the body that he gets to see unfolded less and less often as the years go by.

This is the fourth woman whose bikini straps the priest has unfastened in public veneration of her bare back stretched over the altar of his portable massage table. I wonder how many more will willingly sacrifice themselves before the sun begins to set.

*

I take a deep breath and dive. One, two, three, four . . . seconds pass and I don't feel Marin's hand on top of my head.

I allow the salt to push me towards the skies.

I stretch on my back and try to sleep.

*

Last year when I first stepped on this dusty shore, I inspired unrestrained curiosity.

'Are you on your own?'

'I am.'

A barely discernible contraction at the eyebrows behind the sunglasses, in which I could see myself, flinching.

'I had no idea that there is a beach in the Old Town,' I interrupted his next question, shaped like a why. I am a local gone on an adventure, not an orphan tourist.

'Yeah, not many people know about it, but it's quite small, so there's no space for everyone anyways. I'd suggest you come early if you want to get a spot.'

I earned Marin's benevolence the following morning, when I flip-flopped down the steep street leading to the beach at 7 a.m.

He and Ivan were having their coffees at the bar table, facing the sea.

'Morning,' Marin mumbled. 'Want some coffee? Pick a spot and I'll bring it to you.'

From that day onwards nobody asked me why. Marin never smiled and his hellos and goodbyes were careless, distracted, as he always had more important things to do than greet me. But sometimes, while doing his morning tax-collection rounds, he stopped under the shade of my parasol to ask how I was, what I was reading, or how I liked living where I now lived, far away.

'It's cold, isn't it?'

'Yes, very. Not too low temperatures, but the cold gets to your bone marrow somehow. It always finds its way.'

'So what keeps you there?'

'The cold keeps me awake. I can think better there.'

'Ah,' Marin smirked. He had figured me out. 'That's why you come back here then. Nobody thinks here. Look at that idiot for example.'

His X-ray vision had detected a violation: a woman, led by a Yorkshire terrier, was standing on the shore, looking at her phone, as the dog unashamedly pissed on the tragic ruins of a sandcastle.

'No dogs allowed!' boomed Marin and rushed towards the ignorant criminal. 'Madam, mind your dog! Now we'll all drink its piss! How is this possible, shame on you!'

'The fish also piss in the sea, but you don't mind drinking their piss!'

All eyes turned to Marin, whose tan couldn't hide the redness rising. Was the lady His divine equal or a heretic about to be struck by lightning?

'Who the fuck do you think you are with your stinky rat on a leash! The fish also pisses in the sea, huh? Very well, very well then. I have an idea. Let's see if your mutt will swim like a fish if I throw it off the pier, there, huh? If it swims, I let it piss all over the beach, on my towel, in my mouth even! How would you like that?!'

The woman was silent. So was everyone else. The murmur of the sea grew louder in my ears, and I felt quiet gratitude. The woman said nothing else but pulled the leash and dragged the dog away, up the street and out of sight.

We let out a sigh of relief. We were in safe hands.

*

I have undertaken another pilgrimage to this shore whose language I speak like a child. I know some words, as they are my mother's, but too much remains foreign. It has become foreign anew. Some of it, a lot of it scares me but also draws me in. I keep seeking it out and it seeks me out too: random words slip into my mouth as I speak in other tongues. It keeps calling me across the seas, from thousands of miles away.

It is hard to tell why I have returned here this year. I try to remember the days before the trip, before the flight, I search for images of packing my bags and looking for my passport. Was I homesick? The word doesn't move me. It doesn't exist in Bulgarian. The feeling is of undefinable and indefinite sadness: I just constantly wish to be elsewhere, wherever I am.

Lying on my back in the water, staring at the sun, I wonder how far the bottom is. It should be near. When I let my toes go, the water barely reached my chest. I don't know how long ago that was, how strong the currents are. Have I moved at all or am I floating in place?

The flag is red again today, and I feel chained to the sand. This, lying here, with open eyes full of salt, is as close to peace as I can get.

*

Two weeks pass and when Marin brings me my coffee as I spread my towel on the lounge chair, now reserved for me with one of

Marin's t-shirts thrown on it overnight, he asks in his usual disinterested way:

'So, how long are you staying?'

I look up at him, confused by the question. Yesterday when I went to the car park to see if my second pair of sunglasses might be rolling somewhere in my car, I couldn't find the car. I had forgotten where I parked it. The car park was packed with newcomers. It looked different and I struggled to find my way, squeezing between the hot metal bodies, getting caught in their sideview mirrors, and breathing in the heat they were emitting long after the sun had loosened its grip. I walked to my hotel, thinking that the sunglasses I had on my head would do: the scratches weren't that bad.

'As long as you'll have me,' I answer.

*

It's Sunday. I have lost count of the weeks, but somehow it's still late August. The summer refuses to leave. Having burnt and peeled several times, I have new skin now and a new life with it. I have given up looking for my car and when I walked across the old town two days ago, I noticed the thin strip of road that connected us to the mainland has been submerged. Nobody seems concerned.

Marin has become stricter. The flag waves blood-red above his head, and the whole beach is reflected in the black of his sunglasses. No movement goes unnoticed, so it's in our best interest to relax in the shade of our umbrellas and stay away from the water. Wading up to your knees from time to time is okay, though. He understands: the sun is strong. He is not a monster.

Every day the population of the beach seems to change. Some faces are now familiar, but there always seem to be new ones. We don't talk, busy with endless entertainment on our phones or immersed in books, but we scoff at each other if we break the rules. I wonder if anyone else has tried phoning the mainland to ask for help. I don't dare to try. It might raise suspicion, make me a target, ruin my plan. I have one chance.

A child, building his hundredth pile of muddy sand, suddenly stands up and releases a fountain of piss into the waves that reach for his feet. Everyone, including his parents lying on lounge chairs in the first row, closest to the water, watches and waits. Marin, followed by Ivan and the massage priest, runs from the beach café, sensing that something unspeakable has happened. As the storm of shouts descends upon the poor child who is now wailing, his face covered with snot and tears, I sneak out from the shade of my umbrella and walk towards the other end of the beach. There are no umbrellas here, only a few towels with red bodies sleeping face down on them.

I go for the cliffs, finding my way across the slippery rocks. The sea is impatient, its waves trying to catch my feet and take me away. I hesitate, but there is no time: I hear shouts and feel the burn of rows and rows of scornful eyes. I sit down and let a big wave embrace me. It yanks me against a rock, taking my breath out, but I push myself away with my legs and start swimming.

My progress is slower than expected. I climb moving hills of water and when they pass, I seem to have barely moved. I had decided to go for the horizon. The mainland is closer, but I know choosing it would mean more of the same: there will be other towns with their own gods, rules, and shores that will stick to my feet.

I don't look back, but I can feel the walrus-god entering the sea: the buzz of the water under the surface is briefly interrupted and changes its frequency.

I kick faster with my legs. I shovel water harder with my arms. But my shoulders and thighs are already burning, my breaths are not big enough to keep me going, my body is ready to float, just float. I stop, close my eyes and turn on my back. A dead fish with its belly up to the skies.

He reaches me, and I hate His touch.

Rodge Glass
RETURN TO 'THE GORBALS'

Levi picked the buds from his ears. Spots of light peppered the blackness above as he arrived back at the Rosewood. What time did that make it? Late, anyway. Late enough to be early. 'Rosewood' was a pretty name for an ugly place. It couldn't be, but the building looked like it was red, and dripping.

Levi pulled down his hoodie and reached for his phone, pressing pause on the new series of *Blood Money*. 'The Ghost', they called him. 'The Ghost'. He repeated the phrase under his breath as an old photo of the family glowed out at him from the home screen. Arm in arm, all holding their flags, at a protest in New York. FREE PALESTINE, said Hannah's t-shirt. JEWS FOR A FREE PALESTINE, said the badge on her jacket. He couldn't stop looking. At waist height, Hannah's daughters Talia and Yael wore the same t-shirts as their mum, all three of their smiles like radiators among the throng. Levi was in the photo, but only just. His smile was partial; he was wearing his own clothes. The time – 03:58 – hovered in the wee space between the girls at the bottom of the screen, this moment clipped and saved back when Talia and Yael still hugged each other, all the time, without thinking. When they hugged him all the time, without thinking.

Forever ago.

Levi's phone flashed: You have 14,271 notifications.

He shivered in the cold of the October night. Swiped the news away.

Levi wanted to turn around, just to be sure he was alone – but instead he stood still, looking at the blood-red door handle. It was best to put tonight behind him. Tonight, the last week, the last year. It was best to forget the whole world. His card beeped, the red light flashed like a dare and the door released itself, letting him through into the narrow, dimly brightly lit space at the bottom of the stairwell. The Rosewood was not a symbol, a sign, or a warning.

It was just a fucking building. It was still, somehow, his home. Levi smiled and nodded at Jimmy from 1B, who was ambling down the stairs. Jimmy was always the same, no matter the time or date. He was a big man. Tall and wide and true. He was exactly the colour he was supposed to be.

'Good morning, Sire!' he called, following up the cry with a deep bow. 'It's going to be a lovely day, when it comes!'

'Nearly here, pal, whether we want it or not. You up early, or late?'

Jimmy laughed. They must have been similar ages. But he lived like he was in his twenties.

'Now there Levi,' he grinned, tapping his pocket with a wink. 'You know I never sleep.'

Levi slipped his buds into his trousers and ran a hand idly over his skull. Jimmy's eyes were outsized, dancing. He'd been having fun. Could Levi remember what that was like? He padded forward a few steps, yawned, then stopped. There was a spot of blood on his shirt. Jimmy dropped the act. Waggled his doobie.

'You all right there, Levi? What's happened? Want to join me out front?'

Levi rubbed his eyes.

'I'm fine. Just a bit . . . Back to front. You know?'

He held up his phone, as if that was an explanation. Jimmy's eyebrows drew themselves together. He wasn't really one for the digital world.

'Oh yes, back to front I know about,' he said. 'Born back to front, that's me!'

Levi saw Jimmy fixing him with a stare. Was he worried? Levi straightened up. Tried to look well.

'Say,' said Jimmy. 'Where've you been? You know what stress is like for the bones. The eyes.'

Levi waved his hands across his chest as if trying to get rid of a bad smell.

'Ach, late nights, early mornings. It's my own fault.'

'Fighting Nazis in the laptop?'

'They live elsewhere too, you know.'

When Jimmy smiled, wee dimples revealed themselves, making him look even more youthful. The man from 1B waited for more, which eventually came.

'It's a year today, that's all. I've not been anywhere, really. Just . . . walking.'

'William?'

'William. And –' Levi waved a hand, vaguely, at the world beyond – 'everything else.' He held up his phone again. 'You know what? I fucking hate this thing. I don't hate much but I really hate my phone.'

Jimmy raised an eyebrow. Waited. Levi wanted to say something real, if it was possible, with all that distance between them. He noticed Jimmy looking closer, as if Levi's true face was in hiding. If Jimmy had planned to lean in, the moment had passed; he was still smiling, though who knows what smiles might mean.

Levi turned towards the open lift, its green light flashing. But at the last moment he swivelled a one-eighty, took a few paces forward from a standing start, then ran over and pulled Jimmy into a bear hug. Ha! Take that, Scottish reserve! He held Jimmy tight, locking him upright in the hug, stopping him from falling over backwards from sheer force of momentum. If Jimmy was shocked, he didn't let on. If he was afraid, he didn't let on. I could somersault a skyscraper, thought Levi. I'm like one of those Olympian gymnasts! All I need is a leotard, a pommel horse, and ten thousand hours of practice. And to be sixteen years old.

At first Jimmy's hands stayed still in mid-air, like this assault was some kind of test – then his shoulders relaxed in the silence. He folded his own arms around Levi in return, soothing the smaller man with a gentle 'Sshh now, you crazy kid', as he pinched a rollup between his lips. The moment went on. It refused to stop, that's how it felt. Levi tried to remember, his face buried into Jimmy's lapel, if they'd touched before. Maybe twice. Handshake at Christmas, that time? Handshake at Hogmanay, last year? It's not much, over twenty years. But they'd shared a lifetime, pretty much. Jimmy knew Hannah and the girls as well as anyone in London. What would he be thinking, now? Did he ever turn on the news? Well, auld Jimmy would hear, soon enough. A brand-new series! Levi, 'the Ghost'! News reaches everyone eventually. Though how could you take it seriously, this kind of news? Levi pulled away, patted Jimmy's firm shoulders, and turned around, wiping his red eyes.

'Go on,' said Levi, 'Smoke in peace. Ignore me. I'm losing my . . . whatever-the-fuck here. My mind.'

As Levi walked towards the lift once more, Jimmy burned at his back. He pictured Jimmy watching him. Then, as if it were a whim, just one of those things you just do, because hey, isn't my life my life? – he started climbing the stairs. He wanted to call out something like, 'Gotta get my steps in!' Or, 'Good route to a heart attack, right?' But if he was going to survive in this new world, he was going to have to learn. You can't spend your life explaining every little thing you do. It only makes you sound guilty. Far better to go around hugging folk, then going about your business. Ach, they'll say, at the Shiva house, after they lower him into the ground, the soil cast onto his bottom-of-the-range coffin in spadefuls by the cousins. A mystery – even unto himself!

'Stay offline now,' called Jimmy, from the doorway. 'Levi! I said, stay offline, right? Ain't nothing on there worth seeing. Nothing but horror and shame and the end of the fucking world.'

But Levi wasn't listening, not to the words anyway. He was already rounding the first flight of stairs, waving weakly as he went. To Levi, Jimmy's voice just sounded like a crackle coming through an old radio. The kind his Papa used to listen to, in Glasgow, when folk still used the word 'wireless'. When, as a young boy, he'd accompanied the auld man to Shule, once or twice a day. Back then, his tartan kippah lived on his head, in bold Saltire colours, sunrise to sunset. Back then, he didn't care who might see. All this, in days when there were no accusations. In his pocket, Levi's phone buzzed once more. It was how the attacks arrived. It had been buzzing for too long.

On the first floor, Levi checked off the names one by one on the last empty page of his old notepad – Singh, Robinson, Steele, Palmer (that was Jimmy), another Singh. He passed each door as slowly as he could bear. The same on the second, the third floor. Burn, Dobis, Adamczyk. Up and down the silent, bright corridors. McMorrow, Gallagher, al-Hamrani. There were about eight or nine apartments on each floor. Some were well looked after. Some looked like shit.

Levi's mind was unwinding.

He yawned, thinking of when the girls were wee. How Talia climbed in to join them during the night, her little feet kicking the duvet off in sleep, no matter the temperature. How her button toes curled over the lip of side of the mattress. In those days, Talia asked him to stroke her foot until she fell asleep, back when he and Hannah were in their first year living together. What had he lost? Was there a name for it? He might never see them again – though you can't think like that and keep your head. Hashem, he asked himself. G-d in heaven, what is coming? Levi rubbed a wet finger over the redness on his t-shirt, making it worse. *Blood Money* or no *Blood Money*, this t-shirt was going in the bin.

On the third floor, one name was different. According to the new sign, Khan in 3.02 was now Hardcastle in 3.02. Levi stood, arms limp, a man facing the firing squad. Face, uncomprehending. Body, stiff. Where had the Khans gone to? These people, where do they go, and who mourns them? He circled the word 'Hardcastle' in pencil in his small notepad – it looked like an impossible word – HARD CASTLE – then slipped the pad back into his jacket pocket, with a shaking hand. I'm full of charge, thought Levi. I'm still alive. Dear G-d, I should make the best of it.

By the time he reached the fourth floor, the climb had emptied him out, but filled him up too. His heart was popping. The fourth floor, the fourth floor. Some part of him was always on the fourth floor. Levi imagined a race, or a fight, was waiting for him there. Though of course: these people don't fight on a stairwell, or anywhere they might lose. They steal into the ring, unscheduled, unseen, in real life or in the comments sections. They do their worst, then leave. It's the same every time. You dance through the crowd, limbo through the ropes. You arrive, ready, fists up by your nose, trained to within an inch of your life. You shout, *Come on then, you fuckers, I'll kill you all!* Only to find the battle is already over, the winner already lifting a belt high, laughing, while floating through the crowd. All that's left is the unmistakeable stench, rising up from the canvas. And you wondering, yet again, how this keeps happening.

Is there something you might have seen?

Is there something you could have done?

As Annie put it, in her way, 'If you kill yourself, then no one else can kill you, right? It's a form of taking control.' Her friend from Rabbinical school jumped from a ski lift to his death, while on holiday in the Alps, a week before their finals. Just climbed over the metal bar and let go. One more senseless death. Their lives were full of them. Explosions, attacks, retaliations, bombings. You can only see so much death before death turns itself into something else. Before it starts to reduce you, to numb you, in some strange, irreversible way.

There was only one more flat to check, the one directly under part of his own. There was no plaque saying William Lived Here. Its plain white door was set back, hiding like a secret between a store cupboard and the stairwell that lead down, the back way. Levi inspected the space, through the letterbox. He had been on the other side of the door, once, when Will's parents invited him in for a drink on the boy's seventh birthday. He'd passed them at the entrance to the Rosewood a few hours before it started. Swing by, said Ben and Fiona. On a whim, he did. Through the letterbox, Levi could see the wee breakfast bar where he'd sat and discussed the football with Ben. He kept looking. He would not cross the threshold of his own place until he'd done these checks. The details, they were too precise. The trolls, they knew too much. Some fucker was watching, and they had to be watching from somewhere. It's cold, thought Levi, looking through the letterbox into William's place. He was trying to focus, to set aside the recurring image. Those yellow eyes, spiralling at the heart of the meme. The eternal star. That nose, with its impossible, cartoon crook. The bearded, manic Jew, sitting on a pot of money. Sharpening his knife. Working up an appetite, for young flesh.

At the edge of Levi's vision was Will's bedroom door. The boy was crazy about outer space, his door full of posters and pictures. The planets, the stars. He remembered one painting Will did: the moon, right down the craters. On the other side of that door was Will's bed, or what used to be. No one had lived here since. Well, why would you? Though it'd make one hell of a hideout. Finally, Levi let the letterbox flap shut. He could make one more flight. The fifth-floor corridor had small lights embedded in the floor. To him, these wee lights looked like cat's eyes. Unblinking, always. Seeing, everything. Looking out, for what you might do next.

Before going inside his flat, Levi did the regular checks. He looked at the three locks – mortice at the top, key-operated bolt in the middle, open shackle padlock at the bottom – and gave it a good shake. The security camera above him looked untouched. But then, how could you know? How could you ever know? Levi looked at the sign on his door: THE GORBALS, the place titled, all grand, like The Gorbals was some kind of large country estate, not what his father had called 'the shithole our grandparents just happened to land in, when they fell off the boat, way back when.' The mezuzah on the side of the door had only been there a year. It still looked fresh compared to the rest of the entrance. Levi reached up and touched the mezuzah with two fingers, then kissed them and muttered a prayer. Someone had been here, he knew it. Something was out of place. But what? The flat was so small. Surely it wouldn't take him long to find it.

First, Levi went to his bedroom. He crouched down, checking under the bed first. He emptied the bedside table, the contents of the cupboards and drawers onto the floor, faster now, with more urgency – swish, flap, whizz, he might have laughed – then moving to the other bedroom, which was quickly dismissed. No one had been in there in ages. Next, he checked the lounge, with its pile of Jewish literature that Shlomo had given him in recent months, a book every week, at their meetings. *Finding the Jew Inside You. Finding G-d. Finding Your Way To Tikkun Olam.* Lots of titles about finding. That, in amongst commentaries on the Torah, books by rabbis and scholars and historians. Some of these books had inscriptions especially for Levi. 'Makes them harder to give away,' said Shlomo, with a laugh. 'When they include declarations of love.' On the other side of the lounge was his desk, where he used to work, back when he had a job. Now, it was loose with old reports and bits of paper. Notes pinned to a cheap noticeboard. Trigger words and warnings. Post-Its related to old cases he'd been following, a year ago and more. Nothing useful. Had anything been moved there? Truly, Levi couldn't tell.

Next was the toilet, then the bathroom. Nothing, nothing, nothing. There was no space anyway, and he didn't know what he was looking for. He picked up a small, circle mirror, the one he bought for Hannah when she complained about there being 'no way to gaze at my shimmering beauty in this godforsaken hellhole!' Hannah, who'd only usually use that word 'beauty' when referring to the face of some smiling Palestinian child, some nameless babe who was no longer breathing. They were always nameless, these children. Just thinking about this took something out of him, something without a name. Dizzy, Levi reached out a hand and accidentally knocked the mirror to the floor. He looked at the fragments on the floor for a moment. Then stepped over them, without making a noise.

Levi drifted back to the kitchen. He started emptying out the drawers, sending colanders, pans and cutlery clattering to the floor.

This made an intoxicating noise, an unforgiveable noise for this time in the morning. The kind of noise you only make if you want someone to come and complain in their dressing gown. Hey dickhead, some of us have work in a couple of hours, yeah? Hey dickhead, what happened to your humanity? Levi emptied the fridge. The freezer. Okay, they probably hadn't been in the freezer, but you never know, do you? He checked the plug points, feeling along the skirting boards for wires, heat creeping across his shoulders as he clattered, banged and thrashed his way around the perimeter. He knew what he was doing but couldn't stop. Khan, Hard-castle. *Blood Money*. 'The Ghost'. 'The Rosewood'. That's it, thought Levi, the dining table overturned. The desk, its papers scattered. Chairs, tipped over. Bins, unloaded onto the kitchen floor. The recycling. The rubbish. The food disposal. Well, *now* it looked like an aftermath. It was sickening to see it trashed. But it was intoxicating.

Standing in the mess, overheating and throat itchy with the smell, Levi kept scanning the flat for evidence. They'd been here. He *knew* it. He did. He pictured mini versions of Brad and Brenda, in balaclavas, scuttling up the side of the Rosewood in darkness. Crawling through the walls. Slipping in via the holes in the air-con, tiny cans at the ready, leaving the locks untouched. Laughing about the 'security system' as their prints danced across the floor. He saw them, in mid-air, unclipping lightweight weapons from their waists. 'Okay, bitches. Let's get to work.' In his left hand, Levi noticed he was holding an ice tray. In his right, his phone. Suddenly, this all seemed very negligent. Like he was painting a target on his own heart.

Vaguely, Levi opened the French windows and stepped out onto the mini-balcony, which Hannah used to call, with a smile, 'The West Wing'. It was all right for her to joke about money. She lived in a different world, and returned to her Penthouse whenever she liked. Levi gripped the railing, which he could do at the same time as touching the window. Without thinking, he dropped the ice tray he was holding. He leaned slightly over the edge, which stood high over a tiny square of paving, far below. His phone buzzed. It read: You have 27,750 notifications. He thought, 'It is the responsibility of all Jews to recognise prejudice wherever they see it, and call it out.' A line of Hannah's. Via Elie Wiesel, maybe. Or Primo Levi. Or one of those other Holocaust philosophers. Every one of them, calling you out for your future hypocrisies. Every one of them repurposed for the new world. Levi thought about leaving a voice note for Hannah, then decided against it. What was there still left to say? She'd made herself pretty fucking clear, and he couldn't bear the buzzing any more. The alerts for *Blood Money* were multiplying like rats. The messages of insult, the messages of support. Who could keep up with it all? Levi wished he'd been born in a Shtetl. He wished he had no knowledge of conflicts in other places, ones he was powerless to stop but which kept coming to him anyway. Beeping. Buzzing. Squelching. Pinging, in the middle of the night. Asking: why don't you care enough? Quite casually, Levi swayed back, took one last look at the picture on the home screen and dropped his phone over the side, in the general direction of the ground. No, he wouldn't climb over the bar and let go. He'd come back through and get on with it, whatever getting on with it meant. He walked back inside, fresh morning air flooding the space. It was a kind of freedom.

And that's when he saw it. At the edge of his vision, their bright red handiwork waved at him, from the centre of Dad's painting of a horse standing proud in its stable. The words, WE ARE COMING, in bright red capitals, covering the horse's tail and hooves.

Of course, Levi thought, laughing bitterly. Of course, they are coming.

They've been coming for thousands of years.

Reyzl Grace
BRIGADOON

for E. R. Shaffer

A think A knew, somegate,
in that first month we war girlfreinds –

We'd passt the nicht thegither,
an it wis sae haurd tae lea' ye

in the morn, cuisten across
yer gowd-strawn bed

like a saunt's cloak on a sunleam
whiles yer ain lay on the fluir.

Ye laucht, telt me object
permanence is a real thing

an that ye'd still be there eftir
ye walkit me tae the door.

As it shut, I cawed
oot, 'An the door eelit

a hunner year . . .' A wis anely
tryin tae mak ye lauch,

but ye reappeart in an instant,
luiken sae sairious,

catcht bi ma vyce afore
the joke, and then ye grint

in that aaber, elfin wey
ye dae that inveets ma tongue

like the clootie wall caws
the cuinyie in a lanely lass's

purse. A wis late tae wark.
That wis afore A'd eaten

thae cupcakes on yer birthday –
afore A'd passt a century

watchin ye draig a fag
an then kythed tae find A'd na

been missin mair 'an a day.
Nou A knaw why

ye walk circles aroond
the flat whan things gae missin,

why yer een wirth til milk
like some Greek oracle

anent the clock, why
ye maist like daena remember

the lingelie whit apens the poyum
ye demandit, an why ye demandit

a poyum, oot aw things,
whan offert yer auchtin. Ye telt me,

aince, that ye war afeart
A wudna date ye acause

ye're a stoner, but the suith
is A cudna lea' ye kis ye're a *sith*.

THE WITCHIN OOR

for E. R. Shaffer

Whan A come throu the door,
the twa gowd rings
ye daena want for wir haunds
hing in yer lugs, an A smirk.

A'mna fasht aboot whaur
ye keep thaim, lue, sae lang
as thare's eneuch tae skare
whan we're thegither. Ye smile,

tell me ye've been daein magick
afore A cam, an A'm deein
tae knaw whit glamourie required
the gowd bikini an the tossles,

but A knaw better than tae speir
at a witch for her saicrets. A daena
come for yer spellcraft
(saufin whit ye've pit on me)

but yer scryin. Yer haunds swirl
aroond the kirstal baw
o ma kist, yer tongue sweels
the quate puil o ma mou;

yet a pairt o me's aye afeart
that the fire in yer een canna
last – that ane day
thare'll be anely ess, spellin

naething. But ilka time
we lay pechin in glitter
an sweit, ye peer intae me,
broun as an eik's croun,

an say ye see us, auchtie
an lauchin still as we dae,
awaukenin tae tea thegither
juist as we will in the morn.

Then ye tak oot yer huips an yer face
leams gowd. Oh, starnie,
ye daena need tae mairy me
sae lang as ye'll stey ma spaewife.

Lydia Harris
MARY DYKES BROWN

1

you overwintered in your mother
took ill under her grey slate roof

it was not possible to keep you
you were torn, too cold, your mother

cupped your head in her right hand
her three-day daughter, wakeful

through three nights, ill at ease
light as your mossy hair, your flight

through the open window
to the hollow shore

2

I meant to say
two feet by one
I meant to say
if they identify
stone or mound
the exact spot
the plot, if they do
from their records
I can take a picture
for you no words
I meant to say
I'll stand where
she was laid

3
and the spring flooded every stem of White Moss
the broken-necked bird, the moss heart, the hurt moss

and Mary Dykes Brown opened her eyes
to the broken-necked bird and the moss hurt

and the spring flooded every stem

REQUEST TO FIFE BEREAVEMENT SERVICES

did they bury her in coal dust under the bing
or in the red gold sand of the bay

or at the foot of her grandmother's rowan
or by the railway line to the clank of a train

was she buried in linen and lawn
between the pillars of the Old Mens' shelter

with a hint of silk or in a Shetland shawl
or a wedding veil in a sanctuary under a little hill

who turned the hard rock into a springing well
forgave the whirling tongues of the dandelions

the distance between the months of waiting
and the hour of her death in blue-black writing

WORDS TO CONJURE STRONG PROTECTIONS FOR WHITE MOSS

moss   you see how I already have hunches
about un-pastured land   you as vessel
of silence with no fence

I am not saying what you must carry
you are the passage I walk
you are your own body's message

tasting earthy   even comets
remember you   there is something here
this is the point of turning

       oh please uncovering moss
       show me the rock beneath

THE KEY IS THAT MARY DIED

and though in the hall there was a pram
it rattled empty as the cradle

the mother rocked

though the father was a miner
went underground with pick
and lamp he couldn't bring her back

though grandfather was a baker
with fired-up stoves, a bakehouse
full of loaves he couldn't make his Mary rise

though the minister dipped his finger
in the blue glass bowl and said the words
they did no good

though there was a mother and although she smiled
and sang the hymns and pinned a blood-red brooch
to her collar

Mary died Mary died in the mother's arms
and her snow-white shawl was hidden
and her name was never spoken

Stella Hervey Birrell
YOUR BACK REMINDS ME OF CHRIST OF SAINT JOHN OF THE CROSS

after the painting by Salvador Dali, displayed at Kelvingrove Art Gallery

The stuntman hanging from the gantry – your back
        underneath my east-light hands –

 your stigmata, the place
the pain began, eighteen years ago,
like rubble, like clasped magnolia just coming into flower.

These boat-building muscles
preserved by roof-spaced climbs into circuitry webs,
lifting the platform, the floor, wherever stalled automation
        crouches,
sweeping the teenagers off their trauma, holding them high
        above the fishing boats and nets.

Galaxy after galaxy of freckles, crossing under my palms,
and just – you. You, and the proximity of your upper back,
        like the painting –
I spark skin together, make warmth, and

your back underneath my east-light hands – the stuntman,
        hanging from the gantry

CHRISTMAS EVE SONNET, 2022

The half-light, 6:30, and here I am,
chopping carrots into soup, then to shop:
squirty-cream-in-a-can, last gifts, strap for
my aching wrist. These toddlers, in light-up
wellies, hold Christmas taut, tight, it is not
for my between-tween-teens: stocking gifts left
stacked on the living room floor, magic swept
up, emptied into dustbin with a shush.
Yuletide is over before it begins,
the bells all wrung out, lists all ticked off, bar
the making of the soup, cutting the cake –
everything boxed back in the garage, and
the baby Jesus falls from his annual
cardboard cattle stall: wants no part of it.

LOST PROPERTY

A velvet jumper with sweatshirt cuffs.
The dress with the golden sparkles.
The dart board we used for a Playmobil space station.
The brooch, and the boyfriend who gave it to me at fourteen.

The dress I wore to my seventeenth birthday party,
bought for me by my best friend and her sister.
A glove, another glove, a third glove.
The way I hugged and kissed my teacher every day, aged five.

The black coat I took clubbing, the night someone
told me you could catch an STD from a toilet seat.
My wedding ring,
later found in a gap between floorboard, radiator and wall.

Two cats: one to the happy hunting grounds,
the other to a neighbour who gave better food than I could
 afford.
Three CDs of Motown hits, left in the social area of the
 psych ward.
A church whose leader felt called to judge.

All four grandparents, one parent.

Two friends (over the wedding),
seven friends and almost a sister
(over the children).

The ball of cells
that never was a baby.
Only found
for three days.

Elisabeth Ingram Wallace
THICK LINES OF SKY AND SCISSOR SHARP SUNS

The 1930s estate was ringed by another estate from the '60s, and then another from the '70s, and another new one, scabbing at the edges, and it was much like living inside the rings of a tree, like being part of a wood-boring infestation, doomed to tunnel our way in circles until we'd eaten out the bones of the place, and the whole city fell down.

Someone had recently vacated the 1930s home by dying, and left behind a house full of dirty orange carpets and a kitchen full of spiders. Some were all legs, others had fangs.

It was also full of ghosts. You could hear them groaning, falling down the stairs and burning pies; they liked to turn on the oven in the night. Turn the toaster up to max. They would randomly boil the kettle or ring the doorbell or flood the basement. They had left behind big steel closets full of black clothes and empty beer bottles, and cigarette stubs in the toilet.

They seemed to be harmless ghosts, because the house was always full of sunshine. The swirly copper, yellow-brown carpets made the whole place bright. Wherever you walked a million skin cells spiked and tickled the air, and it was hard not to sneeze and cough and hear the ghosts laughing, passing through your nose, scratching in your mouth, curling question marks in your hair.

There was a glasshouse outside, hot soil and dead flies cooked in it.

The dead flies lay on their backs, little legs up in the air and had gold bubbles for eyes. I could see the clouds, floating inside them.

Mum didn't have a new boyfriend yet, and that was vast and peaceful, and so except for watching the flightpath send white stripes and rumbles through the sky, there was nothing to do but make crank calls and watch the pond for goldfish.

Next door had a giant rottweiler puppy in their garden, she was soft and gentle, and crammed in a tiny cage by the bins. Her face pressed tight against our metal wire fence and her wet nose poked through the holes, and I'd go out every day and kiss her, and pass her an ice-cream cone, let her lick my hand with her hot pink joy.

My grandfather came by sometimes, in the sky-blue car. He'd fill the house with sweet pipe smoke, coil candy smells in the air, and send Kazka running up the stairs to get me. He'd bark until he found me, then sneeze.

Of course, they both felt the ghosts at once.

No one else felt the heavy corners kicking, or the shifts in light, the cracks in the night.

The ghosts liked to jump inside our brains so they could smell the darkness of mould and the poisoned rats under the floorboards, and walk once more with flesh, all about their old home.

We would feel them, entering us in our sleep – their brains, inside ours, their dawn dives, their cold night swims through our lives. Kazka would fight them in his sleep, with growls and snarls and snaps. I would let them run through my bones. I was too tired to fight what was already in me.

By the time we left that house I knew one ghost well, an old lady from the ice who had died falling down our stairs. I knew her favourite seaside café, all her heartaches and best recipes for herring pie and pickle soups, plus I had learned Icelandic and gleaned the entire plot of the Saga of Finbogi the strong. There was much mystical talk of ice and Thor. Often, I would wake up and think *Mörk bauð eg mundangs sterkum, mannni, tyggja ranna, Grásíma skaltu góma, glóðspýtis það nýta, Iðrast muntu ef yðrum, allráðr flóða úr sjóði, lætr eyðanda líða, linns samlagar kindar*, and then have to get up, brush my teeth, and go to school.

It is hard to stumble through the Lord's Prayer when your head is full of thorns.

My grandad smiled whenever he visited us, and he chuckled whenever he saw me. He could see the many months of ice-fishing with ghosts was taking it out of me. He could see I'd been snow-bathing and tree-climbing far away in the past, pickling rollmops and gathering dead jim dandies from some strange tree.

I told him my real mother was buried under a juniper forest, and he nodded sympathetically.

He was the one who would slice an apple and give a small part to me, and leave the other lump on a side table, so it could go brown and the ghosts could enjoy the vapours and leave us alone for a few hours.

And so, the dead passed through the '30s house in brief possessions and bruises that gathered in the night. Nothing extraordinary, although I often had dreams that lasted days, once I spent a year inside a school of cod. I was a silver shiver, swimming in wrinkles of light. Then I woke up, ocean still crackling in my head.

I'd dread falling asleep, gripping that white horse, rip tiding away. Who knew how long I'd be taken for? You don't know how long a month can be until you have migrated the Barents Sea.

I did mention it briefly to my mother. She thought I had a brain tumour and made me see our local doctor. He said it was not unusual for a child to see shapes in the sky, *clouds do sometimes have fins*, he winked.

Just an active imagination. She'll grow out of it, he said.

The ghosts and ghouls and fairy tale phase. Too much television.

We were not in that house long, much less than a year, maybe just one long hot summer, or alternatively, forty-three years, if you go on old-lady-from-the-ice time.

My mum ignored me, my brothers ignored me, and the ghosts mainly ignored me, if I left them a few slices of apple and kept a light on all night.

In the end, I only communicated with the rottweiler next door. That was true love. Each morning, and each night, her tail wagged at my approach, and she yipped with pure bliss. For one summer, each day began and ended with a kiss through a silver cage.

Whether it was a long time, or a short time, it was time, and I kept on waking up inside it.

Every day, an ice-cream van sang outside, circling the estate, coughing fumes into our open windows. Sometimes I'd run out and buy a treat.

That whole summer I had ice inside my head, headaches and Jumbo Rockets, Ninety-Nines, and raspberry syrup the colour of nosebleeds.

That whole summer was one long crank phone call, with one voice and no end. I'd wake up on the stairs, holding the big beige telephone, not sure who to call out to. There was a stranger in my head, a shrill voice shouting in my ear, *Hello? Hello? Who is it? What do you want? Who are you?*

Then came autumn, and the new school year.

My classroom was close enough to the kitchens to hear the water screaming to a boil, and the dinner ladies laughing, and dropping teaspoons on the floor. Sealed inside September, the rain steamed the windows into mist. Ferns waved black outside and spat birds. Our breaths condensed us inwards, towards the blackboard: hot, and mute in the boiled cabbage air. I drew isosceles triangles in thick white chalk. I multiplied. I divided. I was seven, and eight, and nine.

I could hear each whack of the knife. The stir of a pot. The smell of their cigarettes, their coffee, the flick of water spitting into fire. Obtuse triangles. Acute. Convex, concave. Oceans, and Queens.

Black hands twitched on a white clock that I could not read, time pointed and spun. Each day was rain and fog, damp noises, pressured screams, bells and hymns, gut pangs and prayer. My job that week was to cut out the planets, then hang them in the sky. I had fishing wire and Sellotape, and the universe was dot matrix paper.

Lunch was Tupperware, or brown circles of flesh, or white circles of flesh. Industrial hunks boiled in bags and gravied and potatoed, with lumps of green, then pink custards with skin, each mouthful a shallow breath of powder or slime. A choke, a bone, a vein. A tick, a tock. Rhythmic, heart beaten.

The worst lunch was roe. Grey slabs of fish eggs, blended and fried into wax. I felt my belly swell, and a million babies dive and burrow, I'd shut my eyes to jump into myself, and a billion tadpoles would pour out of my mouth, in streams of steam, explosions, out, out my eyes, my nose, stainless, and silver, each fish dropping teaspoons on the floor.

I was always the last to be picked up at home-time, but this time was different.

The class and the teacher went home. The cleaners went home. The caretaker was gone, off somewhere in the carpark, smoking, burning boxes by the skips.

It was her dad's turn to pick her up, my mum said later to the police, *it was her mum's turn*, my dad said.

I put my head on my desk and swam. My desk was old and tired, wooden, heavy lidded, beaten, brailed, finger trailed, but inside, it smelled fresh and empty. Like sweet things chopped down. It spiked my skin with splinters.

Inside, were my things. My lesson notebooks, my coloured pencils, two sharpeners, a large pot of wood glue, a rubber frog, a painting of a sparkled Christmas tree. I breathed it in, filled my chest with forest and flight and silent night, holy night, all is calm, all is bright.

The glue tasted like vinegar. My protractor was sharp and brought out a lovely full stop of blood, each time I stabbed my hand.

While I waited to be collected, I cut out a thousand bolts of gold lightning, and then a thousand more. I put them in my pockets. Then I cut out a school of silver cod and ate them. Then I cut out the sun, and bled punctuation all over it.

Sharp vinegar twists in my gut.

My glue was for glitter, for sunsets, for Christmas, for thick lines of sky and scissor sharp suns. My glue was to stick sparkles in rainbows, a dense opaque, that would dry sheer to a shine, and varnish anything in perfect, frozen, under snow-white slime.

It blobbed out the tub in a loud bubble. It splurged in a gob, I rubbed it into my palms, my nails, my knuckles, my arms.

Then I glued my lips shut.

I didn't care that the glue was made from the bones of dead horses, boiled up. We'd been told that once, gleefully, with smirky disgust, by a teacher, when she saw that some of us liked to eat the macaroni necklaces we made in our infant year; hard pasta, covered in glue and sprinkled with glitter. She wanted to stop us eating our craft projects, but it only made me want to eat more art.

You are what you eat.

I'd heard enough fairy stories. I might yet grow hooves and equine magical powers.

The circle on the wall kept moving. The silence was silver, and tadpoled, and had hands.

I glued my desk shut. Then I glued desk after desk shut. Then I walked the halls. I walked around the school, sticking the doors shut, gluing the windows shut, then the toilet seats, then back to my desk to stick down the sky, the trees, and the planets. I stopped the solar system from swinging.

Eventually the caretaker came to lock up.

I walked down the rainy street and sat on the pavement outside a pub, peeling off my glue skin, shedding like a snake on the tarmac, watching the drunks and nutcases, spin and fall.

Later, punching. Later sirens.

I'm still there. It's getting dark.

I can't open my mouth.

I'm a picture on a wall, brass tacks in each corner. People rub their fingers over me, but it's not clear yet what I am, this picture's not dry.

I've got a lot of lightning in my pocket. Vinegar in my gut.

Horses run through my bones.

Karen Jones
STRAW WOMAN

My sisters have made a scarecrow that looks just like me, dressed her in our dead father's clothes, sat her in a chair in my room with a spare straw beehive wig on the chair next to her for the days they want her to look more like our dead mother. They find this almost as hilarious as they find me. I know they want me to rage at them, for my face to flush, my hair to escape its fixings like angry straw, but I am comforted by this life-size effigy, can imagine it as one of our parents' spirits come to visit my room, where a real beehive hangs from my ceiling, its inhabitants more confidantes than my sisters could ever be.

I sit beside the scarecrow, hold its dry hand in mine, and memories spill out of me like so much stuffing. Our mother left us once, drove off with a man in a red car. She wore green feathers in her red hair, a pink frill on her blouse, and had dabbed the last drops of her expensive perfume on her wrists and neck – we had never seen her look so pretty. The man had an oversized cap and a strong jawline. Our father had no car and no strength to fight for her – too busy managing the farm and his wild daughters. And wild we were, untameable, like the red curls we inherited from our mother. We had none of our father's traits – not stoicism, not quietness, not duty. We ran barefoot in fields, caught tadpoles in jars, hid the hares he wanted to destroy – pests, he called them – letting them multiply until there were too many to hold and hug and hide, brought home stray dogs that were not working dogs, so only more mouths for him to feed, lured feral cats to join our menagerie. Our mother encouraged our behaviour, brought more useless animals of her own to the house.

Our father gave up. 'Let it all go to hell,' he muttered.

And since they both died, that is exactly what has happened to the house – animals of all kinds live with us now. Even the farm animals are welcome inside. We know our neighbours and our workers talk about us, call us mad, but we love our animals and we love our falling-down house and we love bringing the two together.

The day our mother left in the red car, she told us the man was a distant cousin, that he was taking her on a shopping trip where she would buy us new dresses and shoes. She was disappointed that we weren't more excited at this prospect, but we hated dresses and rarely wore our shoes. We were happiest in our underclothes, breathing free and easy, muddy and mischievous. She shrugged, told us to look after Father while she was gone. Our father did not go to wave her off, to speak to her companion, to tell her he'd miss her. She was gone for three days. Father looked surprised when she came back but asked no questions. He tipped his hat in her direction and went back to work in the barn, though his gait was less steady and his shoulders rounded. When we asked why she had no shopping bags, she waved us away with a sigh, took off her coat – no frills or feathers in sight, the sweet perfume replaced by stale sweat – put on her apron and made dough for the next day's bread. She never mentioned the outing or the man she said was her cousin again.

When we cleared out our mother's things after her death, we found two masks in her old trunk. Masks meant to be worn to a ball. When we were small, she told us tales of dances, ballgowns, diamonds, orchestras, feathers in her hair, but she never mentioned masks. They look like one is male and one female. The male mask has black feathers and a long beak-like nose, while the female mask is all reds and golds and cat-eyed. We pictured her in a fine gown, her curls springing around the mask. She must have been beautiful – even more beautiful – when she went to that ball. After the trip with the man in the red car, she never spoke of the past again and when we nagged her for bedtime stories about dancing with fine gentlemen, she shushed us and read boring stories from books written by people we didn't care about.

My sisters sometimes wear the masks when we are baking. They do this to annoy me, know I will complain about the masks being damaged, covered in flour or the juice from berries. Sometimes I hate being the eldest, hate that I have had to be responsible, had to become more like our father, while they get to remain as versions of our mother. Yesterday, while I tried to clean the few parts of the house not filled with animals, they called to me to come to the fields, to hurry, their voices filled with excitement. I ran, afraid they were in danger. They pointed to a cow in the field in front of the house, a crow on its head.

'Look! The crow is like a fascinator, the cow is ready to go to a wedding,' Esther said. She and Livvie collapsed in a heap of giggles.

And I wanted to yell, to say, 'This is why you called me?' To tell them that they had interrupted my work – work they never help with – but the joy on their faces was infectious and I couldn't help but smile at the thought of a cow at a wedding. Another crow arrived and sat on the cow's back.

'That's her plus one,' Esther said, and we all laughed together. I should do that more often. I should let them remind me what fun life used to be before the fire.

After our mother died, our father could only find one photograph that hadn't completely burned. At her funeral, he gripped it in one hand and tried to gather us up with his other arm, but we were too big by then for him to capture us all at once and he let his arm drop to his knees. In the photograph, our mother was smiling, wearing her work clothes and apron, young – before we were born – but the part of the photograph that had been scorched away had stolen her hair. She looked odd without her curls framing everything – her face bigger, her eyes wider, her nose flatter. At the graveside, he dropped the photograph on top of the coffin and we cried, wanted to keep it, the only photograph we had to remember her by.

'It's not her,' he said, 'without that hair. It could be anyone, but not her.'

We wanted to argue, to fight, but we knew he was right – she was not herself without her hair and he was never himself again without her.

He kept going, for us, we supposed, until I was old enough to look after my sisters properly, then one of the workers found him dead in the far field, his eyes closed as though finally sleeping peacefully, five crows sitting on his chest, as if protecting his heart from anyone who might dare try to restart it. We found no surprises in our father's things, no hidden life from before our mother, no dance shoes, no fancy suits. He was exactly as he presented himself to the world – a good man, a diligent worker, solid and true. And no match for our mother.

Beneath my window, my sisters play fiddles and sing our songs and laughter floats up and swirls and birls around the scarecrow. The bees buzz their own song above my head. I lift the scarecrow up, take her in my arms, a faint scent from the clothes she wears conjures up my father, and we dance. But no magic brings her or me to life. I place her back on the chair, put the beehive wig in her arms so she can whisper to her imaginary bees. Tomorrow, she and I will wear the masks and imagine leaving this place in a red car. We won't tell my sisters.

Allie Kerper
SEXT AFTER THERAPY

Come over. Bring your hammer.
Smash the projector in my head.
Pose with the debris
in your dykefag tank top –
what can I say? You bit my dictionary
and it's all oozing instinct.

My turn. Stroking the haft's grain
I map deep time, extract fossils,
dust them off to puppet your myths.
My red pen sheds its carapace,
soaks through your latex gloves.
Sniff my new name on your fingers.
Slap me if I start to pretend
we're not pretending.

Which of my fluids will turn you translucent,
translingual, quoting the poetry
of Pangaea's fissures? Grab my hand
and pick a crack to jump into.
Let our entrail prophecies
fuel theses on future planets.
None of them will know the word for how you look at me
holding that hammer.

ASMR GIRLFRIEND MUTUAL ATTENTION VIGNETTES STREAM OF CONSCIOUSNESS (SOFTSPOKEN, RELAXING)

Easy as the sun's finger slipping
through a gap between curtains
you unclick the latches
on my suitcase skull,
lift me out, tease each crease
to oblivion.

You hold me like rock
holds a river, sturdy
as boundaries blur.
My movements carry
grains of you glinting,
growing the bones of what lives in me.
A welcome softening, you tell me,
emancipating space
you'd thought solid.

Pass me that knife.
Close your eyes. There,
that's the lid carved
and twisted off. I extract seeds
from your goo like ancient coins
whose effaced emperors lack
language for their worth.
Let me scoop out that gnarled string.
You're a smooth stage
for my lighter click's echo,
the danse de vivre of flame.

Marcas Mac an Tuairneir
EITHNE

Às dèidh Leabhar Mór Leacáin

Tro lìth nan ùillean, brisidh
cruth do chuirp, a' sgoladh tro
linntean flodraich do Bhearramaine.

Glèidhte san tionndadh 's an uchd
an t-srutha, fo thrìd-shoilleireachd
dhuilleagan a nì a sìor-shùghadh, tha

Brìgh do sgeòil is brachd banail buill
do bhodhaig ri biorgadh, sultmhor
mar bhric-shàile aig ìre tilleadh lànaich.

Do bhroinn ri èirigh, na cruinneachd
choileanta, tha lainnir a fliche fo
sholas-là – ach,
                    do leòn na gheòb,
a' leigeil gaoir a streafan fèith is feòla,
fogharach san fhànas on d' reubadh gille.

Chan fhaicear do ghnùis – a-mhàin:
duibhr' a sgiabail mu ìochdar an uisge,
ruaidhe do gruaig ri snìomhadh an uillt.

EITHNE

After the Great Book of Lecan

Through the film of oil, your form
emerges, sculling through the eddying
centuries of river that bear your name.

Clutched in its turn, in the thick
of its flow, the limpid pages drain
your narrative of its essence, rich

In womanhood, your limbs flex,
speckled like trout, full and ripe
in the flux of fertile return.

The globe of your womb rises,
drenched and glinting under
daylight – yet,
                          the wound, a mouth
of flesh and sinew strata, wails, echoes
fill the void from which a boy was ripped.

Unseen, the features of your face – alone:
its writhing in the water's blackness,
your auburn hair in the river's twist.

COILLE GHALLAIBH

Às dèidh **Landnámabók** *is* **Laxdœla** *saga*

An doimhneachd na coille
   toradh m' inntinn
thig cruth air mo smuaintean
   's craobhan air leagadh

Plaosg mo chnarra
   plodaireachd giuthais
gach geal dhèile
   mar chliabh Amhlaidh

Gabhaim ma cùl
   cùrsa fom làmh-sa
bheiream sùil ghorm
   air tìrean bu ghoill sinn

Grian a' teàrnadh
   air tonnan a tuath
folachd a' chuain
   mar chridhe Þorsteinn

Bogha mo shiubhail
   ri fàthach Thìle
bhuam mo rùn
   bonntachadh bhràithrean

Air cladaichean Arcaibh,
   's Eileanan Chaorach
ìghnean mo mhic-sa
   an caidreamh an iarlan

THE FOREST OF KATANES

After Landnámabók and Laxdæla saga

In the depths of the forest, is the fruit of my mind. My thoughts finding form as the trees are felled. The hull of my knárr is a buoyancy of pine. Its every white plank like the ribcage of Ólafr.

I'll take its rear, steer the lines from the keel. Cast a blue eye on the lands where we were foreigners. As the sun descends on the northern waves, the ocean will be my lineage, bloodied like the heart of Þorsteinn.

The arc of my journey now focuses on Iceland. My purpose far from me in the homesteads of my brothers. On the shores of Orkney, and in the Faroes, my son's daughters will lie in the embrace of their jarls.

MAC-MEANMNA

Às dèidh Eleanor, Ban-dhiùc Ghloucester

B' i an eiriceachd meadhan
a brathaidh, seach an eucoir. Ach
gun chomraich Westminster,
ghabh i ri tèarmann an eilein —
dàn ris nach robh dùil

Fiù 's tro fhoghlam na draoidheachd seo
is bàs a' feitheamh oirnn uile fhathast,
bu leòr mac-meanmna, gun
dearbhadh rùin.

Am b' urrainn dhaibh innse le cinnt
gum b' ann na ìomhaigh rìoghail a bha i –
no a cuid fèin, air ath-laghadh
an cruth banrigh?

Cha b' e feum fiosa,
ach beachdachadh a-mhàin
air na dh'fhaodadh a bhith ann,
a' fàisneachadh dìomhaireachdan
ciùin is caochlaideach
de dh'fhigearag cèir.

IMAGINATION

After Eleanor, Duchess of Gloucester

Her heresy was the means
of her treason, not the crime. Still,
denied Westminster's sanctuary,
she acquiesced to that of the island –
a destiny unforeseen

Even by way of this learned magic.
Yet, death awaiting us all,
imagination sufficed, with no
evidenced intent.

Could they say with any definity
it was in his royal image –
or her own, remoulded in the
visage of a queen?

It was not the need of knowing,
simply envisioning of what might have been,
divining the mute and mutable secrets
of a wax figurine.

AN CAOLAS

Às dèidh Carolina Oliphant, Bn-uas. Inbhir Narann

Mhair tùs nan òran
na dhìomhaireachd eadar peathraichean:
cuspair air a chagarsaich gu aon taobh
an seòmraichean-cuideachd dhaoine mòra

Ach, fhathast nan sileadh-sùith
tron chàrr, chaidh an seinn le càch
an taighean-leanna a' Mhìle Rìoghail

Agus mar sin,
nuair a thugadh iad, am beòil shiubhlach
thar a' Chaolais, air an ath-bhreith
far an do chruinnich Albannaich

Chan robh gin aca den bheachd
gum b' ann na mac-meanmna-se
a chinnich a crann-caorainn
gus an do chuireadh air ais a rannan
fo bhuaidh-aithris fhireann, air an gabhail
a-rithist, far an do leig iad ciad fhreumh.

Mhair na h-òrain, fada às dèidh
a h-èirigh don nèamh –
a-nis air an ath-chluinntinn, chithear a fìrinn.

THE NARROW SEA

After Carolina Oliphant, Lady Nairne

The songs' origin
remained a secret between sisters:
the subject of sotto voce asides
in society drawing rooms

Yet still they percolated
though the haar, sung by others
in the alehouses of the Royal Mile

And so, when carried
in itinerant mouths
across the Narrow Sea, to be
reborn where Scotsfolk gathered

None presumed
it was in her imagination
her Rowan Tree first bloomed,
until its quatrains, sent back
with male attribution, were again
performed, where they first took root.

The songs remained,
long after her ascension
to the Land of the Leal –
now re-heard, her truth is seen.

Donnchadh MacCàba
ÀS ÙR

Oiteag
mhìn, shocair
ach geur is fionnar
gam dhùsgadh le anail bhlàth a beatha
a' leigeil aoibhneas ma sgaoil,
a bha fo ghlais fad
sìorraidheachd.

AFRESH

A soft
gentle breeze,
yet cool and sharp,
awakens me, the warm breath of her life
setting free joyousness
imprisoned for an
eternity

SGÒTHAN

Latha lainnireach geamhraidh,
sgaoth nan eun-tràghad ag èirigh
air a' ghainmheach aig oir na mara
is a' seòladh seachad os cionn nan tonn,
sgòth dubh an aghaidh a' chuain chiùin
ach an-còmhnaidh air astar bhuam.

Fuar, fuar is stoirm air fàire,
san ear bha a' ghealach ag èirigh
san iar a' ghrian a' cromadh,
nuair a nochd sgòthan ioma-dhathach
air iteal àrd sna speuran sìmplidh gorm
nan cruth mar sgaoth de gheòidh shàmhach.

Ann am marbhan na h-oidhche nam shuain,
stoirm de dh'ìomhaighean ag èirigh,
bruadaran buaireasach gun soilleireachd
fo sgòthan dorcha m' inntinn,
is a' tuiteam is a' bristeadh
air clachan a' chladaich chorraich.

Christopher Whyte
ANGELS

1
I have always envied the angels
for not being subject to the savage division
into genders, for staying seductively
somewhere in the middle regions

between men and women, so
we have no way of knowing if the desire
they awaken in us when we look at them
is lawful or unlawful, sinful or permitted.

Will they continue to represent the ideal
of bisexuals until the end of the world?
I'd love wings to grow on my back
that would lift me mightily into the air

without any need for pushing with my feet,
to carry information here and there
and gather secrets which could serve
as matter for the divine gossip of angels.

2
If I were to succeed in becoming an angel,
I wouldn't withstand temptation. Once I'd alerted
Abraham to the presence of the ram,
afterwards I would talk to his son,

calming him, reassuring him, but also
scrutinising the shapeliness of his body,
his shoulders and the down above his lips.
I would explain to Tobias how he had to use

Crìsdean MacIlleBhàin
AINGLEAN

1

Bha farmad agam daonnan ris na h-ainglean
a chionn 's nach fheudar dhaibh dealachadh borb
nan gnè fhulang, oir fanaidh iad gu mealltach
an àiteigin sna raointean meadhanach

eadar na boireannaich 's na fireannaich,
air dòigh 's nach eil fhios againn am bi 'm miann
a dhùisgeas annainn, 's sinn a' sealltainn orra,
laghail, neo-laghail, dligheach air neo peacach.

An ann gu là luain a thaisbeanas iad
sàr-bheachd nan co-mhiannach? Bu thoil leam
nan robh sgiathan a' cinntinn air mo dhruim
a thogadh gu neartmhor san adhar mi,

gun fheum sam bith air putadh le mo chasan,
naidheachdan a liùbhradh an siud 's an seo
no dìomhairean a chruinneachadh, gu bhith
'nan stuth aig gobaireachd dhiadhaidh nan aingeal.

2

Nan soirbhicheadh e leamsa fàs 'nam aingeal,
cha sheasainn ris na meallaidhean. 'S mi toirt
fios gu Abraham mu làthaireachd
an rèithe, bhruidhninn le a mhac 'na dhèidh,

ga chiùineachadh 's ga chur aig fois, ach cuideachd
a' sgrùdadh eireachdas a chuim, a ghuailnean
òganail 's na gaoiseid mìn os cionn a bheòil.
Dh'innsinn do Thobias mar a dh'fheumadh

the heart, the gall-bladder and the spleen
of the giant fish, at the same time
suggesting we could spend a night together
in bed, before he departed on

his mission to free Sara from her demons.
Arriving to tell Mary the peculiar
conditions under which she could get pregnant,
I'd ask what she was reading when I came.

3
Angel of death, or else of passing over,
when I approach you with the personality
that was mine in this life, each quality
and feature, laid out on my extended arms

like a beloved garment that I won't
be needing any more – will I get the chance
to tell you what was lacking, the hopes
that remained inarticulate, unfulfilled?

Will I have time enough to complain
that I didn't learn about or experience
love in appropriate measure, that doubts
persisted concerning how human I was,

how truly similar to others like me?
Will I have to hand back the golden,
lovely tool of art that was my saving?
Will you explain what sense all of this had?

cridhe, adha 's domblas-àigh an èisg
aibhisich a chleachdadh. Sa cheart àm
thairginn oidhch' a chur seachad le chèile
anns an leabaidh, mun do shiubhail e

airson Sara a shaoradh bho na diabhlan.
'S mi dol a dh'inns' do Mhoire cùmhnantan
neònach a leatruim, dh'fheòraichinn ciod e
'n leabhar a bha 'na làmhan nuair a theàrn mi.

3
Aingeal a' bhàis, no an ath-cheumnachaidh,
's mi dlùthachadh riut, leis a' phearsantachd
a bh' agam anns a' bheatha seo, gach feart
is fiamh, càirichte air mo làmhan sìnt'

mar aodach gràdhaicht', nach cuirear gu feum
nas mò – am faigh mi cothrom bruidhinn dhut
mu dheidhinn na bha fàilligeadh, gach dùil
a dh'fhàgadh neo-fhoillsicht', neo-choileanta?

Am bi gu leòr a dh'ùin' agam gus gearan
nach robh mi 'g ionnsachadh no fidreachdainn
a' ghaoil gu ìre iomchaidh, 's teagamhan
a' fantainn ann mu cho daonnail 's a bha mi,

mu mheud mo chleamhnais ri mo chosmhailean?
Am feum mi inneal òrdh', àillidh na h-ealain
a thoirt air ais, a rinn mo shàbhaladh?
Am mìnich thu a' chiall a bh' aig sin uile?

4
Perhaps you will merely touch me gently
with your powerful staff. All at once
whatever feelings I had will start to fade,
and the new conscience I believed

was going to be long-lasting, like a high
wall that has been whitewashed, but someone
looking at it still makes out the blots and
cracks that distinguished it in days gone by –

will it be blotted out in a blazing burst
of light so painful, so annihilating
you'd think the whole universe had been destroyed?
Will our separation from the personality

that was ours in this world of appearances
truly be so sad – was it a short-term
solution only, an interim way of saying
something until the right words could be found?

5
I never took part in the furious round dance
of eternity, never tasted the haughty,
superior flavour of total knowledge,
informed beforehand what is going to happen,

the start and finish of our enterprises.
What need would there be for Michael
to measure on unsteady scales of judgement
the good and evil deeds each soul committed

4
Ach 's dòcha nach dèan thu ach beantainn rium
gu macant' leis a' bhata chumhachdach
a th' agad. Bidh gach faireachdainn air ball
a' lagachadh, 's a' choimseas ùr – a chreid mi

gum biodh i maireannach, mar bhalla àrd
a chaidh a ghealachadh, ach chìte fhathast,
is neach a' sealltainn air, gach smàl is sgagaid
a chomharraich e anns an àm a dh'fhalbh –

ga dubhadh às an spreadhadh lasrach leòis
cho ciorramach, cràidhteach 's gun creideadh tu
an cruinne-cè gu lèir bhith air a sgrios.
An ann gu dearbh cho muladach a bhios

ar sgarachdainn bhon phearsantachd a bh' againn
ann an saoghal nan taisbeanadh – fuasgladh
diombuan a bh' innte, dòigh air rudeigin
a chantainn mus lorgadh na faclan ceart?

5
Cha robh mi riamh a' gabhail pàirt an ruidhle
dàsannach na sìorraidheachd, no feuchainn
blas uailleil, uachdarach an uile-fhios,
a dh'aithnicheas ro-làimh na bhios a' tachairt,

tòiseachadh is ceann nan oidhirpean.
Dè 'm feum a bhiodh aig Mìcheal subhailcean
is droch-ghnìomhan gach anama a mheasadh
air meidhean cugallach a' bhreitheanais

if everything was settled in advance?
Angel, you are merely a go-between!
However tottering and foolish my
view of things, I believe the angels

gather around us to observe
and to take notes, following
our misguided, faulty undertakings
with an amazement that can never ebb.

6

> *Jüngling dem Jüngling*
> —*Rainer Maria Rilke*

Angels' non-binary nature was a constant
headache for whoever painted them!
The naked torso of the one who's at
Tobias' side offers no hint of breasts,

his right hand indicating which direction
they should go in, his left grasping the fingers
of the young lad with the monster fish
whose innards have the power to cure his father,

also to put Sara's devils to flight.
His delicate head is round like a ripe peach,
his hair the same red colour as his cloak,
concern and curiosity mark his profile

while the angel turns towards him, grave
and meditative. If it weren't for the wings,
huge and fluffy, adorning his shoulders,
you'd take him for a slightly older youth.

Northern follower of Caravaggio, 'Tobias and the
   Angel'

nan robh gach crannchur suidhichte bho thùs?
Aingeil, 's e eadar-mheadhanair a th' annad!
Air cho faoin, neo-chunbhalach 's a bhios
a' bharail agam, creididh mi gu bheil

ainglean a' cruinneachadh mu thimcheall oirnn,
gar sgrùdadh is a' gabhail nòtaichean,
a' sealladh air ar gnàthachadh mì-threòraicht'
is mearachdach le iongantas nach traogh.

6

> *Jüngling dem Jüngling*
> —*Rainer Maria Rilke*

Bhiodh measgadh-gnè nan ainglean a' sìor chur
nan dealbhadairean truaghant' 'nan cruaidh-chàs!
Chan eil lorg de chìochan air com rùisgte
an fhir seo a tha trèorachadh Thobias,

a' sealltainn dha le làimh cheairt iùl an astair
fhad 's a tha làmh cheàrr a' glacadh meòirean
an òigeir, a tha giùlan an èisg mhòir
leis an sgudal a dh'fhuadaicheas na diabhlan

's a shlànaicheas athair. Tha ceann Thobias
cruinne, fìnealta mar pheitseig mheata,
is fhalt ruadh mar as ruadh dath a chleòca,
oir-loidhn' aogais làn neònachais is cùraim,

an t-aingeal a' tionndadh ris gu dùrachdach,
trom-chùiseach. Mura b' e na sgiathan mòra,
peighinneach a sgeadaicheas a ghuailnean,
dh'fhaodadh e bhith 'na fhleasgach na bu shine.

Neach-leantainn Charavaggio o thuath, 'Tobias agus an
  t-Aingeal'

7
Look over your shoulder. The fraudulent old man
you so long believed you represented –
nothing but emptiness to be found in the place
he habitually occupied. A new explanation

must be devised and put to the test.
He is no longer relevant to the question.
Don't place too much faith in the stolid image
of a father, so similar to those who are

protagonists in this timebound world of ours.
You wretch, news never reached you
that God had died, that you and your companions
in the undercover corps had been forsaken –

spies in an enemy country, used
to getting information and guidance
from the far-off, authoritative voice
of mobile phones that all at once stopped working.

8
Angel, don't place too much confidence
in the reach of the powers that are yours.
I have a privilege which you enjoyed
only long ages past, at the beginning

of your journey, when you had to choose
between two squads – those who lost the struggle
and were cast down into eternal fire
and those who operate today

7
Seall thar do ghuailne. 'M bodach meallt' a chreid thu
gum b' urrainn dhut a riochdachadh ro fhada,
cha do dh'fhan ach falamhachd san àite
far am b' àbhaist dha bhith suidhicht'. 'S fheudar

mìneachadh ùr innleachadh 's a dhearbhadh.
Sguir e de bhith buntainneach anns a' chùis.
Na cuir cus dòchais ann an ìomhaigh stòlda
athar, is i ro choltach ris a' chuid

as deanadach san t-saoghal thìmeil seo.
A thruaghain, cha do ruig an naidheachd thu
gun deach Dia bàs, 's tu trèigte còmhla ris
gach companach a bha nad bhuidhinn dhìomhair –

spiothairean ann am fearann nàimhdeil, 's iad
gu h-àbhaisteach a' faighinn fios is stiùiridh
bho ghuth cian, ùghdarrach am fònaichean-
làimhe – a sguir air ball de dh'obrachadh.

8
A h-aingeil, na bi cur cus earbsa ann
am farsainge nan cumhachdan a th' agad.
Tha sochair agam nach robh thus' a' mealtainn
ach linntean cian' air ais, aig tòiseachadh

d' astair, an uair a b' fheudar roghnachadh
eadar dà bhuidhinn – cuid a chaill san strì
's a chaidh a shàthadh chun nan teintean sìorraidh,
is cuid a dh'obraicheas an là an-diugh

as messengers, supplying help and comfort,
while I walk unsteadily along the sharp
blade of having constantly to choose,
every pathetic undertaking of mine

altering the delicate balance of the globe
which proceeds on its axis with the demure,
steadfast gait of a princess going to meet
a suitor who may prove to be a monster.

9
(It's said that they used to keep –
together with the banners and the mantles
decorated with tassels and gold,
the imposing hats and fruits of every sort

with which they could adorn
the corners of a painting, or other places
that risked being left vacant or defective –
broad wings forming part of the equipment

of any decent, active workshop.
No one remembered which was the bird
they had belonged to, or where
it had been caught. They were used

for depicting angels. A young lad
who slept overnight in the place
insisted he had seen them lift and fly
through the darkness with steady, powerful beating.)

mar theachdairean, a' toirt furtachd is cobhrach –
fhad 's a tha mis' gu cugallach a' coiseachd
air faobhar geur an taghaidh leanmhainnich,
gach oidhirp fhaoin a ghabhas mi os làimh

ag atharrachadh claonadh mìn na cruinne
air aiseal, a dh'imeas le seasmhachd mheata
bana-phrionns' a' dol a choinneachadh
ri suirghiche a tha, math dh'fhaodt', 'na uilebheist.

9
(Thathar ag innse gum biodh iad a' cumail –
còmhla ris na brataichean, na cleòcan
sgèimhichte le babagan is òr,
na h-adan flathail, measan de gach seòrsa

leis am b' urrainn dhaibh oisnean an deilbh
no àiteachan eile a dh'fhanadh falamh
no easbhaidheach a dheagh-mhaiseachadh – sgiathan
farsaing' a bha 'nan roinn den uidheam aig

gach bùth-obrach deusanta is dripeil.
Bha a' chuimhne caillte ciod e an t-eun
ris an robh iad a' buntainn, no a' cheàrn
san deach a ghlacadh. Dh'ùisnichte iad gus

ainglean a dhealbhadh. Dhearbhaich gille òg
a chuir aon oidhche seachad anns an àite
gum fac' e iad ag èirigh, 'g itealaich
tron dorchadas le bualadh neartmhor, sàmhach.)

Scott McNee
UP BEINN CHABHAIR

They stopped by the lochan to rest and stop the bleeding.

Much of the hike had been bog-ridden, almost impossible to reckon with given the heat. Cathal looked across assortments of mud pools, boot-traps and the odd detritus of ancient trail. He could not understand why the sun had not hardened the terrain and cracked the mud dry; why he was hiking through arid deadland instead of a swamp with aspirational delusions. He stood upon what he took to be the chine of a path and watched string-limbed insects skim the surface of the water.

Come to think of it, he could not understand much that had occurred recently. His reason for being on the mountain was elusive enough, as were the contents of his pack – padlocked through the zipper – and that was before he forced himself to contend with the stabbed man who was currently sitting by the water's edge, breathing hard.

The stabbing itself was no mystery – Cathal remembered driving the knife in (just left of the sternum, biologically; behind the Beinglas Campsite toilets, geographically) if not his motivation. Perhaps the man was someone he had seen before – at the pub the night before, among a throng of rasping tourists. It was equally possible, Cathal supposed, that he himself was a tourist, and the wheezing but nonetheless dogged hiker was an unfortunate local.

He left his pack on a lichenous rock and took a few steps forward into the lochan, drawing in a sharp breath at the sudden cold at his angles and suddenly – absurdly – remembering a newspaper story about dry drowning; people crumpling dead at a touch of cold water. He stood a moment and decided he was still alive. Odd, how the newspaper headlines could flash through his mind and not, say, the names and faces of his parents. He dropped his hands to the water. It took several attempts before his palms were clear of the fetid mud sloughing from his boots.

'Water's still,' said the man on the banks. He was reclined on his own bulbous backpack, red and ruined belly pointing upwards. 'Don't drink still water.'

Cathal straightened up, perfectly symmetrical twinges of pain at either side of his lower back. 'I can see the streams that feed it.' He pointed, feeling oddly impotent. 'Running water.' Despite this, he waded over to the feeder stream before he cupped his hands and drank.

The stabbed man oscillated momentarily, as if he were an overturned beetle. Eventually Cathal decided the man was searching for the mountain's peak.

'You won't see it,' he said, 'even on a clear day. This place folds in on itself a million fucking times.'

'Have you been here before?'

'I don't know.'

'Me neither.'

Cathal came out of the water and slumped on the bank, no longer concerned about the muck. 'Do you need water?'

'Don't think it'll do me any good.'

'Neither did hiking for two hours.'

The man let out a short, huffing laugh. His bare stomach was curiously bloated, despite not being a large man by Cathal's reasoning. If he suddenly stamped on that belly, what would come out of the mouth? Blood and air would be anticlimactic rushing out of that skin drum. The man drew a flask from his open coat and splashed a dark liquid around the area of his beard. He shuddered and twitched, followed by the same liquid, barely diluted, rushing from the wound in his midsection.

'You had that flask the whole time?'

The man coughed. 'Just realised I had it.'

'Have you remembered anything else?'

The man shook his head.

'Me neither.'

Another huffing laugh. 'Should we focus on what we do know?'

The man was right, their conversation tended toward the tedious. Cathal looked back at the water-skimming bugs, wishing for a frog or songbird to snatch their absurd proportions from his vision. Did they slide a proboscis across the water, more medical equipment than animal? At least let them come closer so he could crush them. 'There are no other hikers,' he said eventually.

'We haven't seen any, at least.'

'Or heard,' said Cathal. 'No wind.'

He heard the man oscillating on his back again, the cloth rustling as harsh a sound in this place as metal scraping metal. 'Occurs to me,' the man said, 'both of us know the way on some level, if we don't know the reasoning?'

'Explain.'

'We've both led at one point. No plans, no maps, not much of a path but we seem to know – know the terrain on some level.' He gave out one of the bloodied gasps that Cathal was long since used to. 'We have packs – a knife.'

'No knife,' said Cathal.

'What?' For the very first time, the man sounded surprised. Even when the blade went in, he'd only exhaled.

'It's not on me. I don't remember what happened to it.'

'We both remember the stabbing.'

'I'm aware – I am not aware of what happened to the knife, so don't blame me.' Then, quieter, 'maybe it's lodged in your fat fucking stomach.'

As if in answer, the man began squeezing his stomach, broad hands spread on either side, hairy knuckles rising up as he gripped the flab.

At first, Cathal had the absurd notion of an animal tunnelling outward, then that someone – Cathal himself maybe – was somehow cutting out from the wound he had caused, the knife inverted in its own tear. The point, now that it had crowned, began to distend from its tapered edge, ragged sides emerging and stretching the wound's slick crater. Just as the object threatened to rip beyond the boundaries of the original wound, the man groaned and spasmed, shaking the object loose and sending it tumbling over his clenched white hands and clattering into the scree of the hill. Cathal crouched by the man, registering for the first time the name Ogilvy on the stranger's torn clothing – brand or surname, he had no idea – before his gaze turned to the stone.

A gastrolith. The stone was smooth for the most part, save for thin ridges at the edges, a brief indication that it had once been part of something larger. Slate-like, brushing his fingers across its surface removed most of the blood on the first try.

He paced the banks of the lochan, asking himself whether something being unexpected necessarily meant that it was significant. Behind him, Ogilvy the prone irritant let out another one of his indeterminate noises, a groan or a croak that bordered on a belch. Cathal ignored him and began straining and craning his neck, momentarily forgetting his own admission that the summit was hidden from them. Observing the hill's folds, he experienced the impression of a memory, an older woman, rangy and whippet-like, running cross-county through the same folds. Another face he had forgotten. But if there were once runners, there might be a hope of rescue.

He considered heading back the way they had come, but the ascent had been treacherous enough – descending it with a slouching, wounded man to his right and a river on his left likely to be spate by the time they reached it seemed unlikely. Besides, something had kept them going this far. The summit was the only thing that made sense.

As if in reply to these thoughts, Ogilvy pushed another rock from his wound, an igneous bulb the size of an infant's head and twice as heavy. It slapped into the grass and scree with utter finality. At the sight of it, Cathal reconsidered the slate-stone in his own hand.

'We've passed no cairns,' he said. Carefully, he walked the path back to Ogilvy, pleased with where his thoughts were leading him.

'What?'

'There should be cairns, or at least trail markers all over these hills.' He crouched over Ogilvy's wound; heat rose rancid from it, enough that in the dark or cold it might steam. 'They're missing.'

Ignoring Ogilvy's whimpers of protest, he reached down and squeezed. A succession of pebbles rushed to greet him, dark and bloodied. Cathal took the largest and began a square base further down the path to begin the stack of his cairn. After several trips back and forth, he noticed that Ogilvy appeared to be dead, or at least diminished in some way; the weight in the man's cheeks and stomach reduced significantly. Cathal could not tell if he was still feeling the man's breath or merely the curious heat from the gastroliths that the corpse continued to produce. He decided that this continued production was confirmation that his idea was working in some way.

The water striders on the lochan became his method of tracking the passing time. The sun remained immobile and to judge by the cairn's slow progression was disheartening and only emphasised the pains in his lower back and the new ones flaring in his biceps. The striders, meanwhile, crossed the lochan in a deceptively methodical fashion – the erratic impression of their movements being nothing more than a clinical performance of furtiveness, to trick whatever might try to hunt them. They covered the lochan bit by bit; rocks slid together with a satisfying scrape.

Strange that they were the only signs of life – as he retrieved more of Ogilvy's rocks from drying blood pools and dead yellow grass, nothing rose to meet him or scattered upon exposure to light; no worms, no slaters, no devil's coach horses affronted and snapping their pincers. Perhaps pesticides had wiped out the hill, first directly with its terrestrial creatures and the avian by proxy. They were long past the height where the trees dropped off, and there was not even the standard highland sight of a dead sheep twisted in a ditch or old fence. Just him, the striders and Ogilvy, if the latter's deflated and pallid form still counted.

He paused and drank from the stream, his teeth aching in protest against the cold. Solo male hikers, or risk takers as he might call them, were the most likely to encounter trouble in these hills. But winter was the worst time for that, and he had enough water here to counter the heat. Only thing to worry about was starving.

Idly, his movements linking the thoughts for him, he brought up a ragged stone and slashed at the fabric of his locked pack, as if food might suddenly spill forward. It resisted him and in turn, he resisted the urge to kick it into the water. Something rattled within; food, or more rocks.

'I don't think that it's important,' said Ogilvy.

Cathal rose to his feet. His panic was muted, as if he were already remembering it years later. This had happened once before – as a child, he had casually stepped out of the way of a dangerously speeding car and felt little but surprise. 'The pack?' he said.

'We had the packs when we came in,' said Ogilvy. He was in the same position as before, speech as ragged as ever. 'I can't say about the locks, but I think that's why the packs aren't important. We're not supposed to access them.'

Cathal half-leapt the distance between them and booted the man in the stomach. The structure of the wound held for a brief moment before it ruptured, failed and cascaded red steaming rock onto Cathal's boots. Ogilvy shuddered and died again. Was that the second or the third time now?

Cathal resumed stacking his cairn. There was no point in regretting his temper or washing off his boots – he assumed now he'd never be rid of Ogilvy.

The cairn rose to his midsection. The bulbous rocks that served as its crooked spine held firm, as did the slates that sprouted out as shelf-like ribs. The heat of the body continued to emanate from them, and smaller looser pebbles seemed in a permanent state of tumbling down the structure's levels, never quite diminishing.

When he stepped back to admire his work, he found another cairn squatting and waiting some distance behind his own. Looking back, a third lurked by Ogilvy's flat, crumpled figure. He walked to the one past his own construction and found, to his great excitement, another cairn waiting beyond that. Some great chain was restored. How did not matter; only that it was done and a path had emerged. Even the sun seemed to have finally moved in the sky, the light now flickering orange over the water striders and their reflections, and briefly over the wet, rubbery skin of a frog that slid into the lochan and vanished from sight.

Cathal laughed. 'Be seeing you, Ogilvy,' he called, and began to follow the trail of cairns.

He did not see Ogilvy and the lochan again, or the summit. Following the warm, breathing cairns, he eventually came to somewhere far worse.

Kevin MacNeil
MORNING IS BROKEN

Light blazed through the window, set the kitchen gleaming. The walls were sunflower yellow. The worktops, pans, coffee equipment and oven shone. My feet, bare, glowed warm from the oblong sun-puddle in which I stood; I felt like a battery charging. The kitchen was still – almost too still. The fridge hummed quietly. A clock tick-tocked. A waft of yesterday's banana bread reached out from a cupboard by the window and softly tugged at my nostrils, glad and hurtful, like nostalgia, something from childhood's far-off galaxy. My heart began to pummel my chest. I realised I was holding my breath. The silence – attentive – made me feel as though someone else were present in the flat holding their breath, too.

A high bell chimed, stabbing adrenalin into my heart. I startled. Only my phone pinging. I exhaled, took the phone from my pocket. A text message:
FIX THINGS
The phone sounded again:
I cry
I shook my head, smiling, and replied:
What's wrong?
Su responded:
I wanna scream. Fix me. Thank.
I wondered how come she was awake before midday, figured she was in bed and would sleep again soon. I messaged:
Meet me outside the arts centre at 8. That thing I told you about is happening tonight.
A moment later, inevitably:
I dunno. Sounds bit boring.
I sighed.
I'm going anyway. Put outdoor clothes on, do some crazy make-up and come along if you feel like it?

She wrote back:
>Rude.

I grinned.
>Back to sleep, Su.
>
>Su: *R u d e.*
>
>*I want coffee.*
>
>Me: *Coffee is the best!*
>
>Su: *I'm the best.*
>
>Me: *Ok. – Su, coffee, literature, comedy, the rest of stuff.*
>
>Su: *Um. You appreciate coffee more than literature? What kind of monster are you?*
>
>Me: *I misread that as What kind of mother are you.*
>
>Su: *Why do you keep reminding me that you're blind?*
>
>Me: *Not blind, just eye disease. At any rate, might or might not see you later, haha.*
>
>Su: *Drinks are on you. Thank.*
>
>Me: *I can do that.*
>
>Su: *If I go and it's boring, I kill you.*
>
>Me: *Goodnight, Su.*
>
>Su: *Imma kill you anyway.*
>
>*Nah, gonna watch a movie and hate myself.*
>
>Me: *Do film part only. You'll prob fall asleep halfway through.*
>
>Su: *Your *face* is asleep halfway through.*
>
>Me: *Later, Su.*
>
>Su: *Maybe.*

I turned on my favourite oven ring and placed the red, double-spouted moka pot on the hob, adding my little yellow stoneware cups, which sat thirstily under the spouts. 'Life,' Yuto Hino wrote, 'is a process of waking up and growing up.' Coffee, therefore, is the most enlightened drink! I didn't know why only tea got a Zen ceremony; I resolved to invent a coffee ceremony.

The coffee, now heated, gurgled and spurted and sputtered into the wee sunshiny cups, dropping, thick and black like oil. The espresso had an aroma of dark chocolate and blueberries, rousing in my mind earthy colours and smells, camping memories, and the feeling of the uneven ground underneath you as you awoke in the soupy air of the tent, cows stirring in the field over by, and pulsing there in the background the marvellous swish of waves cleansing the shore, the very sea your young self would shortly be running towards in joy, whooping as you crashed into the gasping purple coldness of the water, so icy it seemed momentarily to stop the heart.

The espresso, too, was a neat shock to the brain, grounding me in my challenging job, rented flat, rented *life*, my effort to be something.

*

Su met me outside the arts centre. I had spent much of the day in a grey funk, turning to Japanese novels for wisdom and for some secret access to self-belief.

Su's face stunned passers-by, attracted stares. Her eyeshadow turned each eye into something like a sunset seen on a better planet – vivid, rainbow-coloured, at once unreal and mesmerising and perfectly as it should be. She gave her eyes wings that swooshed and faded as real birds might transfix the attention while they swooned gracefully towards the horizon, or rather, like sumi-e depictions of such birds, more yearningly stylised than actual birds. Su had suffered from acne – more precisely had suffered from bullying centred around her acne – and had taught herself how to be a high-calibre make-up artist, which is how she made a living.

'Your make-up is an absolute sensation,' I said, and beamed. It cheered me to see her like this: not only the artistry of what she did, but her indifference to what others thought. She created such make-up wholly for herself, applying it when she chose; she often stayed indoors all day, yet would sometimes paint her face elaborately despite the fact no one would see her.

'Wait,' she commanded, holding a finger up. 'Burp.' She scrunched her face, gurned, swallowed. I knew this routine. She was trying to summon a burp.

'Remind me which charm school you went to,' I said.

'Shit,' she said. 'It's gone.' Her face registered a palpable sense of loss.

You couldn't tell Su what to do – she would certainly do the opposite – so I tried to hint by saying, 'Did I mention why tonight felt important?'

'You mentioned buying me drinks.'

'I just feel . . .' I paused, looked at the building's entrance, shook my head. 'Everything is losing its essence. Everything's flat. Predictable. Pointless.'

Su made a face and 'mimicked' me, a thing she did. This involved putting on a childish, wheedling voice and parroting my words back at me: 'Everything's flat. Predictable. Pointless.'

'Very good,' I said drily, unable to avoid smiling a little with my eyes. Her playfulness always got me.

She laughed. 'You love it.'

'I really don't.'

'What is this thing anyway?'

Su took little-to-zero interest in other people's lives. I had already told her about tonight. Twice.

'I've already told you about tonight. Twice.'

'Meh, I wasn't listening.'

'Comedy showcase event. A small number of comedians get to perform in front of agents and TV folk and the general public.'

'Comedians? As in "me me me then some more me"?' Her face fell. 'Why do you hate me. That bar better be well stocked.'

'I don't even know if this will cheer me up, like if it's the right thing to do or the wrong thing.'

'Your face is wrong.' She grinned. Then off my look, she said, with mock sympathy, 'Your face isn't wrong, it's just alien-looking.' She smiled again. 'Aw, you want pat?'

Su patted the top of my head hesitantly, like I was a dog undergoing flea treatment – this was another thing she did – and said, 'Pat, pat.'

I watched this nook of the world. The city streets seemed charged with possibility and the fact that this hurt, hurt. Cars zipped past on eager engines, people knowing exactly where they needed to be and how to get there. Couples sauntered along, arms around each other's shoulders or waists, dawdling to any happy old place. Maybe happiness could bring its own serendipity the way hard work brought luck. How I wished to make a difference. I saw in all this dynamism things I lacked – direction, purpose, a sense of fitting in, a worthwhile contribution. A bus heaved past, with its beleaguered human cargo, jaded faces staring unblinkingly out the windows. How to help them? Else, why be here?

The moon shone in the sky, full, glorious, mesmerising. She was so bright you could make out her details in 3D, not the scuffs and scratches of a lesser moon, but the actual craters among which some humans once drove golf buggies and performed nonchalant longjumps.

'Cool,' I said, 'how the moonlight is sparkling off your make-up.'
'Yeah?'
'Yeah. Cinematic. Let's go in.'
'This better be good,' said Su with a look of friendly warning.

*

The auditorium was vibrant; a diverse blend of people thronged, manoeuvred – chatting, glancing surreptitiously at the entrance, gesturing, laughing. People being people. Only, some of these weren't people so much as tickets to a better future, and the desperate comedians knew it – you could tell by their frantic, sycophantic body language.

Someone tugged at my sleeve but as I turned round – it was Su – I noticed a tall man in a tailored suit had done or said something to get her attention and she was blurrily wheeling round at the same moment I was. Did he look familiar? Friend of Su? Had we met? After a few indecisive moments, I sidled closer.

'... you a drink?' he was saying.

'Yeah,' said Su. Abrupt. Assertive. I wished I had her confidence.

He moved off to the bar, people making way for him either because of his height and suave, imposing presence, or because he was somebody.

'Hey,' I said, 'that guy who's your new friend –'

'How many times? I don't have friends.' She wasn't entirely joking.

'You have me.'

'Yeah, and you're an alien.' She glanced over her shoulder. 'Him? First thing he said was basically how important he is.'

'What's his name?'

'Can't remember.'

'Is he an agent?'

'No, some bigshot at a TV production company.'

'Introduce me! I'm going to tell him a funny story.'

'Nope.'

'You've got to! Maybe that's why I'm here.'

'He's a sleazebag. Plus, how can you introduce someone whose name you don't remember.'

'He's coming back!'

He returned with two large glasses of prosecco, barely registering my presence, or wilfully ignoring it.

'Here you go,' he said, handing a glass to Su.

'Cheers,' she said.

'Here's to you! You didn't tell me your name?'

'Nah,' she said. 'You asked if you could get me a drink, not if you could talk to me.' She raised her drink and, tipping her head back, downed it in one. She handed the glass back to the suit while disdainfully turning away from him. He took it from her reflexively, but his lips tightened into a ferocious grimace and his cheeks flushed scarlet.

I died a minor death. I shrugged, mouthed 'Sorry', but he was already skulking coldly away.

'Su,' I said. 'What if he wanted to give me my own TV show?'

'Shut up. Go and get me a decent whisky.'

When I came back with a large dram, she already had a glass of whisky in hand.

'Where'd you get that?'

'Some guy. Asked if I wanted a drink and I said "No", and he got me one anyway. Tosser.'

I frowned. 'Don't tell me he was some TV producer.'

'So he claimed.'

'What?'

She grinned, took the glass from me. 'Just messing with you. He was a bigger nobody than you.' She handed her empty glass to a bewildered stranger and looked about contemplatively.

'What are you thinking?' I asked.

'So this is your tribe.' Her tone was unimpressed.

'No,' I said. 'I don't belong anywhere. But even if? I mean, what of it?'

She pursed her lips. 'I just wonder what the purpose of someone like you is in the gene pool. Then I remember you're from another planet.'

*

Su twitch-twitched at my sleeve like a mischievous shadow come to life. She was a little drunk, doing it to be annoying. I pushed the doors open and stepped into the night. I wanted to lie down in a park and stare up at the moon.

'That was *shit*.' There was anger in her voice. She was right. As the doors swung shut, she dragged me a swaying step or two to the side and pushed me against the concrete building. She was talking at me, complaining about how terrible the comedians had been. All I could think of was the F. Scott Fitzgerald story about the man who has been gone for ten years, and we wonder if he has been in prison, but it feels like that isn't the case; the marvel with which he feels the solidity of a building after being drunk for ten years is how this feels, a moment in time so physical and pure it collides with eternity, as if eternity grew impatient and needed to hold on to something for support. I wanted Su to smash my skull against the concrete.

Maybe this kind of life, like reading widely, leaves you with a deep and unbearable array of selves. So many worlds, infinite palimpsests, dizzy with meanings.

'I heat things and put them on plates for people,' I said. 'Literally serving the people. That's how I earn my place in the gene pool.'

'We take with us who we are, wherever we go, whatever we do, moron,' snapped Su. 'Pull your stupid self together.'

'I'm going home.'

'I'll walk you and talk sense into you.'

I shook my head.

She stared, eyes devastating. 'You're *going*, just like *that*?'

I hesitated. 'I am.'

A hot branding tool sizzled into my cheek. That's what it felt like. Took a moment to register – Su had slapped my face, open-handed, hard. We both gawked at each other.

Su gave a horrified sound like a strangled laugh, bemused and anguished at the same time. 'You deserved that,' she said, justifying it to herself.

My cheek glowed, nerves flaming and throbbing. Felt like the left side of my face was swelling already. I really didn't understand what was happening.

A moment passed, time doing its thing, neither of us sure what to do.

I nodded. 'I need to be alone.'

She looked into my eyes. 'I think you should be anything but alone.'

My skin crackled. I had a vision of myself as a sentient kitchen appliance, pictured myself in the kitchen at work, a chunk of living meat slicing pieces of dead meat, complicated slave to the machines around me.

She took my right hand in her left and rubbed her thumb softly in tiny circles on the palm of my hand. I missed a breath. My heart's electricity ricocheted wildly.

'I reckon you're okay, asshole,' said Su. She was nervous, something I had never seen in her before. 'Even if you are some sort of alien.'

Suddenly aware of how weary my body was, I retrieved my hand. Nothing was right today. I felt failure all around and very deep within me. The city was quiet now, like something from an apocalyptic movie. How we fail, I tried to tell myself, is how we transform. Su's hand slipped back into mine, cold and perfunctory, like a cat's paw. The night was pitiless.

Su said, 'Name one thing, dumbass, that you're grateful for.'

I didn't feel like thinking or speaking. But I thought for a while and said: 'Morning. Everyone should have a favourite time of day; it means you are guaranteed to experience it every day.'

She snorted. 'Mornings are overrated.'

'Nights out are overrated,' I said cautiously.

'Your face is overrated.'

We both laughed.

I said, 'This was one failed, unfunny night.'

Su looked at her phone. 'It's morning already. Two in the morning.'

'Morning has broken,' I said.

'Morning *is* broken.'

'Morning is broken,' I agreed. 'Your text messages were funnier than the comedy I was listening to today or we went to tonight. The aroma of coffee is better than the taste. What the moon does with the sun's light is better than what the sun does.'

'This is all very profound,' said Su. A pause. She sang the first line of 'Morning Has Broken' loud, into the night.

'Morning *is* broken,' I heard myself saying. 'But maybe it's all about kintsugi. You know? The Japanese method of fixing things with lacquer and gold powder? Like, they fill in cracks in ancient teacups with these fine lines of gold.'

'I know what it is, dumbass.'

'Because they consider a breakage part of the object's history.'

'Yeah,' said Su, 'the Japanese treat objects as people.'

'So – idea. Let's go to a park and wait and see if a golden line of dawn becomes the kintsugi that fixes things.'

*

Dawn, yellow-gold, worked its earnest kintsugi. A marvellous mundane occurrence. It did something to me, traced delicate patterns in my faulty mind. Su enjoyed 'our kintsugi dawn' and, drowsy, got a taxi home to sleep all day. I strolled home to get ready for work.

The sun was shining through my kitchen windows like a joyous spotlight. I made a double espresso. My kitchen vibrated. An illusion, perhaps, created by the weird pseudo-serendipity of sleeplessness and caffeine buzzing through my system and the humming and pulsing of the fridge and other appliances in the kitchen. The yellow walls mesmerised me, an eye bath of warm cheer. Their yellow spoke of beaches and sunlight and bliss. Nature. But the freezer and washing machine and fridge and oven, all of which gleamed with a whiteness that should have offered purity, seemed cold and not just clinical but robotic – callous machines that kept me in my place and made demands of me (feed me, empty me, clean me, do it just so and do it regularly). I was a sentient meatbag on an alien, malevolently intelligent planet. A tourist who got dangerously lost.

The sun shone through more intensely, brightening the room further. The yellow of the walls and the espresso cup popped and leapt with an irresistible mad rapture. The room glowed and my breathing levelled, and I smiled and my lips tingled with salt because a little tear had escaped unnoticed and its tang mingled on my tongue with the warm blueberry aftertaste of the coffee, sparking off it like electricity.

Kathleen J. Marshall
THE SUM OF HIS MISFORTUNES

Robbie takes hold of Arrow's collar and pulls her out of the pathway of the oncoming pushchair. There's something in the thickness of the leather, the clutch of his hand against the animal's neck that gives the illusion there's still stability to be found in the world.

The woman with the pushchair passes, smiling tightly, as he steps off the kerb to make way. He turns his head, fearing the affront of his own face. He's been staring at his reflection in the bathroom mirror for most of the morning, pressing fingers against flesh in a useless attempt to remould his features. Too much of him is not his own. The chin, that nose, the burnt-out eyes. His mother's skidding glance had confirmed as much as she slid his apple juice across the kitchen table, intent on keeping her distance from him now.

His stepfather had been no better, talking too loudly, making extravagant offers to cook French toast for breakfast, his mannered gestures and rictus smile reminiscent of the actors from the amateur dramatics. In the end, Chris had left early, with some excuse about meeting clients, they both knew didn't exist. His sheepish smile was apology enough as he backed out the door, leaving his briefcase behind.

Robbie didn't blame him for going. His mother had hauled the whole house apart in the night. He'd come downstairs to the remnants of her wedding dress, shredded photographs, and old postcards scattered across the floor. *You'd sleep through a bloody hurricane*, she'd told him, filling more black bags with a growing ferocity. He could tell from her tone, and from the crackling silence that followed, there lay the accusation of something far worse than oversleeping. It was there, hovering in the air, ingrained in his intractable features, and smelt like every piece of bird he'd ever brought home for her, now roiling in the bin, slowly thawing.

He walks on, counting out his steps, trying to keep himself rooted to what's in front of him. The pavement, the lamp post, the dog's sodden flanks – his mind tries to latch onto each in turn. A moment's distraction is all it takes. A stray thought and he'll drift into disaster. Arrow scrambles up the grassy bank, snuffling as she goes. He follows, oblivious to the onset of rain, and the newsagent's board parked on the street.

He's reading the headlines before he even realises. The same words he's heard repeated on the television news. This time, they stand on display for the whole village to see. And slowly, understanding begins to seep into him. This is not just something that's happened on the screen in the privacy of his home. It's happened everywhere. It's real.

Twenty-four, the newsagent's sign says. Twenty-four dead, in total. Inexplicably, Robbie starts to hope there might still be one more. The woman with the bullet in her spine, still unconscious in the hospital, or a body they might yet discover in the vast grounds of the school. The tidiness of the number would make it all less believable. Twenty-four deaths add up to one for every hour of the day. If there were twenty-five, Robbie at least wouldn't have to face them all today.

He shakes his head, wanting no part in what he's wishing for. But the idea won't let go. It doesn't mean anything, he tells himself, it's just a thought. And a thought isn't doing. Although, he wonders, as his hand reaches for the newsagent's door, how else does doing start?

The bell on the door clatters behind him, and Robbie's eyes are immediately drawn to the wall of newspapers on display. If he needed any further confirmation of what's happened, it's there, right in front of him. He finds himself staring at the newsprint, and then at his feet. His mother has always told him that any situation he encounters can be risen above. That the mark of a man is what he gives his attention to. But when he looks up, the newspapers are still there. And they still have his attention.

MASS SHOOTING IN PERTHSHIRE
MANIAC KILLS 24, THEN BLASTS HIMSELF
BLOODY MASSACRE IN SMALL SCOTTISH TOWN

He feels a heat spread out across his cheeks as he notices Mr Borthwick staring at him from behind the counter.

'Bad business that,' Borthwick's false teeth click against the words.

Robbie averts his eyes, not wanting to engage, and instantly finds himself swarmed by the same image splashed across the front pages, of a police officer bending his head, apparently in tears. It takes him a moment to realise that the repetition of it lessens, rather than amplifies the effect. By the time he's reviewed all the newspapers, he feels almost inured to the policeman's pain and wonders if he's faking it. His eye hovers on the fortnightly *Stirling Times*, out of step as always, with its front page of a red-haired man winking at a tabby cat, beneath the caption: NEW MOUSER FOR DISTILLERY. Robbie tries to hold onto the image of the cat as he reaches towards the fridge for a can of juice. He lifts the can into Borthwick's view, before gulping back the lemonade.

The sugar lightens his head in one quick thud. He can feel the fizz in his gullet reach up behind his nose and begin to make his eyes water. He turns his face away, conscious that Borthwick is settling his elbows on the counter now, in readiness for a dispute. Robbie tips the can to his face again. If he's drinking, he can't speak. And if he can't speak, then there's no point in talking to him.

Borthwick's in no hurry though. He rings up the newspaper, the lemonade, the roll of black bags Robbie's been sent out for, and then he takes his shot.

'Invercrannan,' Borthwick says slowly, and the name no longer sounds as it once did, 'Bonnie wee place, is it no?'

'Don't know,' Robbie wipes his mouth and shrugs. It's the third lie he's told that morning. The first was to his mother. The second to himself. Words aren't deeds though, no more than thoughts are actions.

'Aye. Bad business. It's the parents I feel sorry for.'

'Parents?' The word feels sticky in Robbie's mouth, the thought of his mother ripping at her wedding dress rears up, the parting in her hair standing out like a long, jagged scar, her face flaming fury, as she asks him the same question over and over again.

'Losing their bairns like that,' Borthwick grimaces, 'A nursery in the name o' God!'

The steady splash of an overflowing drainpipe smacks against the silence and Borthwick leans in closer, the smell of fried fish rising from his breath.

'I hope that bastard rots in hell!' He slams the till shut, closing Robbie's eyes with it.

When he opens them again it's to the thump of coins landing on the folded newspaper between them. He looks down.

DID YOU KNOW THE KILLER?
Phone our hotline: 0840 920 1234

Mobile calls charged at £1 per minute, costs may be higher where you are

Borthwick's eyes follow his, and narrow, as he watches Robbie's shaking hand retrieve the coins one at a time. It seems to take forever. As he picks up the bags, and then the paper, he sees his fingers are already blackened by its newsprint.

He turns and hurries for the door, the clatter of its bell thudding him back out onto the street, where Arrow capers towards him, her tail swatting his legs. The dog circles, her mouth smiling widely as Robbie unties her, rubbing at her back.

'Good dog. You're a good dog,' he says, swigging the last drops of lemonade, before throwing the empty can into the bin.

Arrow doesn't have to do anything or be anything to be good. She doesn't have to lie or not lie. She doesn't have to talk to people, or ignore them, so they see her in a certain way. She just *is*. The sheer simplicity of her, striding along beside him, staring up with her soft, eager gaze, begins to make his eyes smart. He wipes his face, ashamed to let her see.

You're too auld to be greetin. A hunter never greets.

Robbie ducks his head, the side of his neck tightening in anticipation of his father's ready hand. But the blow doesn't come, and he starts to count his steps again, intent on blocking out the growling voice. The rhythm of the count and the dog's steady trot keep the worst of it at bay: the pictures of the nursery, the schoolboys' photos, their parents' crumpled faces, that sobbing policeman. For the first time, Robbie begins to sense these are more than just frozen images recycled by the news, these are actual people who, just like him, were going about their business that day, walking along the street, calling in for a newspaper. They had no idea what was about to happen to them.

Arrow cuts ahead, down the hill, and he follows. Soon, the pavement will run out and they'll have to go back. Return to the chaos of the stifling house, his mother's broken stare, and the thawing stench of all the kills he's ever had a hand in. He'll give her the black bags and try to help her clean up. Maybe together they can eradicate every family photograph, the souvenirs from long-forgotten seaside holidays, all the mementos of who they thought they used to be.

Then it occurs to him that he might just as well keep on walking. If he sticks to the road, eventually, he'll find himself in Invercrannan.

Both options seem utterly hopeless.

'It's okay,' he tells Arrow, blushing at the lie. He claps her back and keeps on walking.

Philip Miller
ON BEING POISONED

I
In the pale photograph,
a girl and a boy in faded cotton among hard boughs,
stand un-poisoned,
walking together on a blue day down the green lane
to the open fields, trees watching, the hedgerow thick as brows,
my sister and I,
spare shoes on our small feet, looking back to where we came,
surprised, our glossy hair gleaming as if wet, as if from the
      river
pulled, but no, we were dry and untouched and young,
and who took our image, who took the photograph
now yellow in its pewter frame, the past long gone, the
      green lane
now gone, but the trees still there, unremembering
that bare day when a girl and her brother stepped on this path
into the sun, into the future now past, this present now, I am
      forgetful,
now we are all forgetful, of who took the snap, who framed
      the picture
of two children alone on a sunny day, heading east from
      the town
into open green country, bare fields, the soil growing
      mushrooms
thick as fruit, wet as hair, fleshly, succulent, brown as blood.

II
A meal like any other,
made in silence, eaten in silence
in the room of shadows,
the piano face snapped shut

where we'd play duets,
her high, me low,
fingers spread,
too small to cover the octaves,

and like the fetid worm of the final day,
the atter was dripped on the omelette,
and we ate, hungry,

and then the fundaments were ruined,
the atomic pattern
refixed and smeared
with spite

and in the dark bedroom,
at three in the morning,
a torrent of flame
and a snake of venom
ejected instead of words
and the flashing blue rippling
on bare walls bent to the ceiling

then stomachs pumped with rubber hands,
an emptying of sense,
a return to the sweet chaos
before time.

And after being pulled dumb
from the warm shadow
with broken teeth, ripped gums,

striations of the lower gut, you know:
this is your life and the lies
of tenderness are over.

*(on the shrieking ward,
half awake, blood faced,
being asked about religion
in case in case in case)*

You can walk again in the green lane,
you can touch the trees, stone and water,
but you are now forever turned,
around your own guts
twisted as a twig,
gyring in the current,
caught up on the low branches,
on the deep side of the sick river,
where the sun lights the far shores:
not yours.

III
Maybe it was some kind of gift
to eat well, and then drift
as deep as the regolith.

Lithe amanitin grow still
in the wet brown mulch.
And once drugged, the body

remains open to sip
a depthless draught again.
In the fields, on the bark,

where the sleep grows,
you can make your rut
and with use and habit

deepen it to a grave
and eat well again,
and lie down in it.

IV
Now and then are in one mind,
the table gone, the house
gone too, lost in the ever mill
of time and distance, and still
we flinch at bright cups of fungi
patched faces, fronds of flesh.
What or who was poisoned?
The boy in that time
or this boy now, looking back
at the sunken path taken since
black with spores
wet with damp,
sweet scent of death caps,
footsteps gleaming with grot,
at night we turn our shoes

and they seep with rot:
all the black footsteps
you have left behind
they lead back
to yourself
alone.

V
If you are betrayed
in childhood,
every following harm,
and loss and leaving,
is half expected,
an unsurprising treason.
If you fall into the arms of death
as a child
you wait, knowing every breath
is a chance to fall again,
there is comfort and fear,
there is choice and warning,
but you cannot unswirl
the blood from the water.
The past is held near
in the present,
and your past fear
has composed the future,
and between prayer and love
reason and unreason,
you suffer the presence
of every dawn.

Victoria NicÌomhair
DEIREADH SHAMHRAIDH

Na coilltean air an còmhdachadh
le criostalan snìomhte
a' deàrrsadh is a' priobadh mar
ulaidh spùinneadair

An uaine na shuain chadail
fhad 's a tha an dorchadas mìn a' fàs,
a' falachadh creutairean na coille,
mar phlaide phàiste

Na làithean màirnealach mar chrìoch fonn
Ràinig am Foghar.

OIDHCHE

Cha ruig cadal ort a-rithist
mar shìol 's a' ghaoith –
sgèith e air falbh gus fàisteal a lorg

Droch aisling a dhrùidh annad
a' losgadh mar lasadh na grèine –
draghan, smuaintean, iomagain,
caraid nach do dh'iarr thu air is
nach leig leat nas motha

Anail shocair mhilis –
Samhradh nad gheamhradh reòite.
Adhlaic thu fhèin anns a' chaladh chiùin,
do chumadh sàbhailte ann an gàirdean do phàrant.

Audrey Niven
MY HEART IS A SUPER-BOUNCE BALL

In the four minutes between the alarm sounding and the submarines submerging in the Gare Loch – as if they could swim away from the missiles – I will grab my denim pencil-case and my troll with the lime-green hair. My brother will come from his class to find me, his socks concertinaed at his ankles from pounding down the hall, and he'll grab my hand and pull me under the desk. I'm sure he'll say it was him that took my super-bounce ball with the Milky Way inside it. He'll tell me I didn't lose it – because I'm not that careless – and I'll still have enough time to say I don't mind, he can have it.

Amy Jo Philip
14.6

This is the wey we enter the scene:
Ah heeze a dram tae the simmer evenin
and, as Ah birl the gless, the crystal
braks the sunlicht intae watergaws,
toatie and fleetin, like a firework display
seen fae miles aff doun the firth. Gin Ah
balance the tummler in ma loof
hou monie years o distillation dae Ah haud
wi this, a malt poured oot tae kirn
a singular year's mind:
the twalmonth reformation o ma flesh.
This is the wey the warld begins anew:
no wi a bang but a whisper,
the cannielike redistribution o the body's
lipid wealth that brings tae licht the truth
kistit ben for decades. Decades when
naebody seen, naebody kent,
when ma ain sel cuidnae awn
the fulness o the life that warsled tae be me.
Thae years when awbody else aroon is
coundied in the strauchle for tae finn theirsels,
they seem tae be fleein doun a motorwey,
straucht and true, when yours is a queerlike gait:
aw hairpins and hill stairts
(walcome tae Bo'ness!)
the steyest o braes, a single-track road
wi jist a puckle passin places
and a thrawn flock o glaikit sheep
the ither side o ilka bend. The truth
sterts oot on its wey no on a lang stracht
like thae roads the Romans biggit ower wir braes

but hirplin roon ae wrang turn efter th' ither,
unco destinations set in error for hame.
Ah wis a muckle time langer in the cask
nor wis the dram nou in ma haun
and the cask is nae braw and hamely place tae bide
but a daurk, dank and doolsome steid.
This is the wey Ah haed tae demature,
tae finn the gait intil ma saicont life.
(Dis ilka trans wumman
feel like this at gey near fifty?)
Pilate speirt o Christ, whase life
lay in the Roman's hauns – mair fragile
nor the whisky gless in mines –
Whit is truth? A better quaistion for the day:
Whit is life? Whit dis it mean tae live?
No jist exist fae yae day til the neist,
at yer darg, yer maet, yer sleep,
but live in aw the fulness ye were makkit fur.
Whit wey did Ah no grund
this life o mines in the truth
afore awmaist hauf a century
wheeched awa ahint me? It wisnae
fear its lane whit thirled me tae bein
the man they cried me. It wisnae jist
the village life, Thatcher's Britain or the kirk
that held me back fae speirin oot
the truth o wha Ah'm are: luve
ey pleyed its pairt in the mixter-maxter.
Luve, whit ettles no tae wound
but in the ettle turns awhing
tapsalteerie and gey near tynes the hail shebang.

Luve's whit apent the cask forby,
unkistit me in aw ma flavours.
Luve's whit let ma tak ma gait
tae lean intil the truth. Tae live.
For aw the sairest o greetin,
luve is whit Ah kirn the day, for wha can lou
her neebor that disnae lou hersel?
Ae time mair Ah birl the gless for tae admire
the lichtshaw it sends oot in kirnin.
Ae swallie mair tae heeze up tae the gloamin
the joy o ma becomin.
Ae thochtie mair tae leave ye wi, dear reader:
Ann an uisge-beatha an fhirinn. Sin an t-slighe.[1]

---

[1] Translation: *In whisky [lit., the water of life] the truth. This is the way.*

Petra Johana Poncarová
CUMHA

Tha dòighean socraichte ann
a bhith a' cuimhneachadh is ag iargain
charaidean is chàirdean a dh'fhalbh,
clann a bhàsaich ro àm-breith,
no anns na ciad seachdainean is mìosan.

Ach tu, a ghràidh,
cha robh thu riamh ach mo bheachd a-mhàin,
agus mar sin, ciamar a nì mi caoineadh dhut?
Càit' am faigh mi cùram agus comhairle
le mo bhròn a tha cho faoin, gun bhunait?

Cha tèid do bhreith,
cha tèid fiù 's do chinneachadh,
air bràigh grianach sa choille,
no, gu gnàthach, san leabaidh aig an taigh,
anmoch as dèidh pàrtaidh le cus fìon.

An toiseach, smaoinich mi:
nach biodh e snog nam biodh tu ann,
pearsa beag air leth, na trì cànain
'nad cheann 's 'nad bheul,
mar a tha iad agam fhèin.

Ach as dèidh sin, mean air mhean,
chaidh e gu ìre eile buileach,
thàinig sannt-ginidh orm
bha mi air mo bheò-thorrach riut,
's tu a' fàs nas fhìre dhomh gach latha.

Thèid corra rud a chall gu sìorraidh bràth,
ach mairidh gaol, is, chanainn, cràdh,
agus chaill mise am fear agus an comas.
A-nis, tha rudan eile a' fàs 'nam bhroinn,
maothran a' chuim gun fheum an àite colann ùr.

'O, na gabh dragh, a bhrònaig,
lorgaidh tu fleasgach eile gun strì sam bith,
agus gheibh thu leanabhan sa bhad,'
thuirt banaltram san ionad dian-chùraim,
's i fhèin cho stèidheil, màthaireil.

Cha tàinig e a-steach oirre
nach robh ùidh idir agam
ann an clann ann an coitcheannas,
ach annad fhèin, gu sònraichte,
annad thar gach mac is gach nighean.

Peanas iomchaidh airson tè
aig an robh riamh barrachd dèidh
air piseagan, chan ann air pàistean,
a bha air a sàrachadh le mì-mhodh,
a bha air a h-oillteachadh ro chiorraman.

Ach bha thusa air mo thàladh
fada bhon teagamh is bhon smuain.
An treòran bhon fhairge,
bu tu mo mhurachan, m' isean-falcaige,
mo thabh-uan liath, mo chuilean dòbhrain.

Chunnaic mi thu anns an eilean,
le spaid is peile air a' chladach
clachagan is sligean 'nad làmhan,
do shùilean sòlaimte, ach do ghàire faisg ort,
mi fhìn is d' athair a' feitheamh riut.

Ach dh'fhàillig mi ort, mo chruit,
tha ar latha dheth seachad,
is chan fhaigh sin cothrom eile.
Siud, a cheist, thoir ort, a-mach leat,
b' e sin an dàn a rinn sinn dhut.

'S coltach gu bheil mi ro sheasg,
ach ma leigeas tu leam falbh,
nì mi mo dhìcheall gus do chur air chùl,
thèid mi a choimhead airson teaghlach eile,
is ionnsachaidh mi sòlas às d' aonais a-rithist.

Nuair a bha mi ag obair air 'Cumha', fhuair mi brosnachadh agus ùrachadh bho bhàrdachd le Nuala Ní Dhomhnaill agus Nuala Watt.

Julie Rea
ASHES TO ASHES

My class all knelt on the crushed velvet cushions; hands clasped in prayer. We were behind the row of nuns, daring each other to pick lint from their habits, our arms darting out like lizard tongues. A boy I liked, Patrick Hennessey, suddenly stood up while the priest was giving the Eucharist Prayer and, with a sly glance to me, yanked the wimple from Sister Mary Concepta. The congregation all gasped and our teacher, Mr Hanratty, rushed across to drag Patrick by the scruff of his neck down the aisle. As he passed, Patrick stared straight at me, a tight, proud smile on his lips, as though he was saying 'I done this for you.' I felt my heart thump underneath my blouse. The nuns gathered around Sister Concepta as she scrambled to put her headdress back on. It was the first time I'd ever seen her hair, it was short, almost shorn, like a grey bird's nest.

Patrick was hauled into the silent room, where the fussy babies and crying toddlers got banished to with their mammies. As Mr Hanratty snapped shut the wooden blinds, it felt like I'd swallowed a stone. A teacher from another class nudged my shoulder, motioning for me to turn to face the priest. Just as he was saying 'Our Father, we say to thee, forgive us, as we forgive,' there was an almighty crack followed by a thud, then Patrick yowling in pain. The priest stared placidly out into the congregation, apparently oblivious to the yelps and screams echoing throughout the chapel. 'Remember,' he smiled. 'Courage is the willingness to be wounded.'

Once it was over, as everyone slowly filed outside, I hung back. As I shuffled down the aisle, Mr Hanratty opened the door, his face the colour of a scrubbed beetroot. 'Aoife Connolly,' he said, smoothing back a forelock of greasy hair. 'Why are you still here?' 'I needed to go to the toilet,' I lied. 'Well? Have you been?' I nodded. 'So ...' He flicked his hands towards the exit. 'Off you go then.' As I passed, I glanced through the gap in the door. Patrick was slumped on the floor, knees up to his chest, blood dripping onto the floor from a wide gash on his forehead. Dazed, I hurried outside. It was too sunny, too bright, and I had to cover my eyes. Patrick's mammy was in front of the main doors, clutching the priest's hand, apologising. The other mammies stood in a half circle, tutting, and whispering. 'The shame of it,' I heard one of them say, even my own mammy, who collected the Bibles after mass and who always said, 'a child is God's greatest blessing.' Just then Patrick, his shirt streaked with blood, awkwardly made his way down the craggy steps. His eyes were watery, and his bottom lip trembled. Patrick's mammy skelped the back of his head. 'My nerves are up to high doh with you boy. You houl yer whisht,' she shouted when Patrick tried to say sorry. 'Just you wait 'til yer da hears of this, then you'll have a reason to cry. A NUN,' we heard her screeching all the way up the street, as Patrick limped alongside her.

I asked Mammy if I could walk home with my best friend, Izzy. 'Aye,' she said. 'But if you're going out, make sure you're home in time for tea.' We took the short cut, the worn trail through the forest beside the burn. As we walked, I cautiously brought up what had happened to Patrick. 'Hmm,' she mulled, her face turned up toward the sky. 'I think Mr Hanratty was right givin' him a tellin' off. You can't do anything bad to a nun. It's a sin.' I let out a long sigh. 'But... isn't it, like, a sin for a grown-up – a teacher, even! – to hurt a kid?' She stopped walking and threw me a black look. 'To hurt a nun is a *mortal* sin. I doubt anybody'll be speaking to Patrick Hennessey for a *very* long time. He's probly goin' to hell for this.' I followed behind, nervously gnawing at a hangnail on my thumb. I remembered how once, during mass a few years ago, I secretly passed sweets to Izzy that I'd hidden in my cardigan pocket before a nun snatched me out and frog-marched me along the aisle to wait in the draughty office for the priest after he'd finished his sermon. As I sat on the cold plastic chair, heart pulsing in my throat, it felt like waiting on God himself to arrive, like some angry store manager.

Daddy worked all week so never came to church. Sunday was the only day he got to have a lie-in. He was sitting at the table, wearing a grubby vest and jeans, when I arrived. 'Oh, here she is,' he grinned. 'That's a great alarm clock ye have there,' he said, playfully jabbing my belly. The overhead light cast a murky, yellow halo over the lace tablecloth as we sat eating supper. Daddy cracked his knuckles, before mopping up the gravy from his plate with a large wedge of bread, as Mammy and I sat in a rigid silence. He propped his elbows on the table. 'Cat got yer tongues tonight?' Mammy put down her knife and fork and smoothed down her blouse. 'If you must know, there was an incident at church, with the Hennessey boy. You know how our Aoife likes him, so,' – she raised her hand to shush me as I started to protest – 'though hopefully not after today and the way he humiliated Sister Concepta.' 'Oh? And what exactly was it the lad done?' Mammy leaned across and muttered into Daddy's ear. He threw his head back and let out a roar of laughter. 'Ah, good fer him. Serves her right. Vicious old bat. Always quick with a leather strap, she was.' Mammy looked on furiously. 'Aoife, go wash up,' she said, before clearing away the plates. 'I wasn't finished,' whined Daddy, trying to grab a pork chop as she passed. I went to my room, their harsh, muffled voices carrying up the stairs. As I lay on my bed, every time I closed my eyes, I kept seeing the blood slowly trickling down the side of Patrick's cheek.

Patrick wasn't at school the next day. Or the day after. It was Friday morning when he eventually returned. We were in the middle of multiplications in Mrs Maguire's class when Patrick, hovering in the doorway, asked if he could come in. She motioned to a seat way at the back. Apart from a thin scabbed sliver on his forehead and a few faded bruises, nobody would've known what happened. But I knew. He walked with his head down now, as though something had been broken inside. The class turned to watch as he took a seat, trying to shrink into the background, trying to disappear. Mrs Maguire clapped her hands together. 'Okay everybody, show's over.'

At interval, some boys cornered him in the bathroom. At lunch, nobody wanted to eat with him. In gym class, we had to pair up and Patrick stood, dejectedly, in the corner. 'Looks like you'll be sitting this one out, Mr Hennessey,' the teacher sniggered. 'I'll do it,' I mumbled, raising my arm. 'I'll be his partner.' Izzy's mouth gaped open. As I made my way towards him, she grabbed the bottom of my t-shirt. 'Are you insane?' she hissed. I shrugged and took my place beside him. Izzy and the other girls glared at me, so we stayed in the corner, away from everyone. 'Why did you do it?' I asked. 'Dunno. I thought people would laugh.' We sat cross-legged on the floor, limply passing the ball to each other. He bit down on his bottom lip, and I thought he might cry. 'It was kinda funny,' I said. 'Yeah, hilarious,' he snorted, pointing to his bruised jaw. At the end of class, as I was leaving, he grasped my hand. 'Thanks, Aoife,' he said, with a bashful, lopsided smile. 'I know that everybody hates me now.' I shook my head. 'Not everyone.' Izzy wouldn't walk home with me or sit beside me in the canteen on Monday at lunchtime. 'Him? Or me?' she said, leaning against the wall outside registration class. 'Sister Concepta almost had a *heart attack* because of him. So,' she eyed me coldly. 'It's your choice?' 'I choose you,' I said meekly.

The next time in school, when Patrick said hello, I didn't answer. 'Aoife?' 'She doesn't want to know you, freak,' snapped Izzy. 'She doesn't like you. Nobody does.' She tucked her arm in mine and smugly dragged me down the corridor. 'Is that true?' he shouted, and I heard the pain in his voice, like shards of glass. When we passed each other in the corridor, he'd search my face, silently pleading with me to acknowledge him. But, like the big fat coward I am, I didn't. After the kids tired of bullying him, they froze him out. He was a blank space, a ghost who walked among us. Rain or shine, he'd eat his lunch outside on the benches. Hunched over. Alone.

*

My granny was a keener. Keeners, usually women, usually in pairs, would cry over a dead person at funerals or the wake and, whether they knew the person or not, would stand guard over them. Mammy said they'd get paid with a glass of whisky. 'The priests got rid of it, of course,' she scoffed. 'They expect death to be a civilised affair. But, in amongst all the pots of tea and sandwiches, the keeners would arrive, screeching like banshees. It was like nails down a blackboard,' she said, dreamily. 'But oh, it made yer heart swell in a stark, beautiful way to hear it. It reminded you that losing a loved one isn't meant to be as placid as waiting in a queue for stamps at the post office.' My granny lived in a farmhouse painted canary yellow with purple hydrangeas at the front door. Patrick's house was directly across from her. I sometimes saw him when I'd visit her, mending the fences or sullenly kicking a football against the wall at the side of his house. One stifling summer day, cautiously pulling back the net curtain an inch, I watched him from my granny's bedroom window. He was in his garden, his back to me, fixing a puncture on his bike. He was bare-chested, sunburnt, t-shirt tucked into the waistband of his jeans. He had a port-wine birthmark on his left shoulder, about the size of a tangerine. I never knew this and seeing it felt like discovering something delicious and forbidden. He was listlessly spinning the tyre when, as though sensing he was being watched, glanced quickly up at the window. I ducked down. I wondered if he'd seen me staring, a surge of electricity rushing through my body. For hours afterwards, I imagined slowly tracing my fingertip around the outline of his birthmark.

*

Old farmer Reilly was driving home after having a few jars at Brannigans Bar. On the blind bend at the bluff, beside the cliffs, he said he swerved when he saw a figure run out in front of him. He was emphatic, someone *ran out* in front of his truck. It wasn't his fault. 'Could drive that road blindfolded,' he said. 'Never so much as hit a sheep in almost forty years, let alone a lad his age.' They found his body about a hundred yards down the road. Only a month before his fourteenth birthday. I didn't blame farmer Reilly. Our fingerprints were all over that steering wheel too.

On the morning Mammy told me he'd died, I was in our kitchen, wearing odd socks and a baggy sweatshirt. As she spoke, I stared at the pulpy bananas rotting in the fruit bowl, withered brown blotches on the stems. They must've been there a while. No-one likes to touch dead things.

*

I remembered one stuffy afternoon, when our class lined up as we made our way to the altar to get ashes. Patrick was behind me in the queue, so close I could feel his warm breath on my neck. The priest thumbed the ashes on my forehead and, as I walked down the aisle, Patrick tugged my ponytail. He was always doing goofy things like that. Izzy was sitting on a stone wall outside with a bunch of girls. 'We're going into town,' she said. 'You comin'? 'Sure,' I shrugged. We ambled down the street in a wide throng. We'd been walking for a while when I got the prickly sensation that we were being followed. I turned and saw boys from class lolling a short distance behind. As Patrick gathered the group into a huddle, I caught his gaze – a leery glint – and felt jittery with excitement. 'GET THEM,' someone shouted. Shrieking, we started to run. As they sprinted after us, I broke off from the group, stumbling down a narrow lane that brought me out onto a marshy field. I hid behind an oak tree and saw Izzy run after Patrick, grabbing his waist, as she tried to kiss him. 'Get off, Izzy,' he yelled, roughly brushing her away. 'Ha! As if I was being serious. You're so ugly,' she said, but her face turned bright red. It was me Patrick chased. I peeked out so he'd spot me, squealing as he bounded down the lane in pursuit. He gently pushed me against the bark of the tree, holding my arms behind my back. 'I've caught you, so you need to kiss me now,' he grinned. 'I'd rather poke my eyes out,' I said. 'But it's the rules?' As he leaned in closer, I felt the weight of him pressed against me, my belly doing somersaults. He wiped away a strand of hair that fell over my face, then licked his lips and closed his eyes. He was about to kiss me when I kicked him in the shin, wriggling free while he hopped around, rubbing his leg. 'You will never kiss me, Patrick Hennessey,' I laughed. He sagged onto the grass, hands on his knees. 'One day I will, Aoife Connolly,' he smirked. 'One day.'

*

'... *we commit this body to the ground, earth to earth, ashes to ashes, dust to dust ...*'

*

It rained the day of his funeral, but the chapel was packed to the rafters. People got dolled up. Izzy, wearing a black bow in her hair, looked distraught, but I'd seen her practising her sad face in the school toilets. Patrick's dad was red-cheeked and reeking of whisky, the bottle sloshing in his jacket pocket. Patrick's mammy stayed at home because the doctor needed to give her medication now. His coffin was in front of the altar and looked the loneliest thing in the place.

Hanratty led the tributes in school at assembly. 'Patrick was a spark plug,' he chuckled. 'A real livewire.' I thought of the faint silver scar on his forehead, the blood dripping down his face. Izzy made posters saying, 'We'll Miss You, Patrick', everybody hugged and wept. Sister Concepta and the nuns spoke fondly of his prank, how they laughed about it still. I felt as though I was sleepwalking through a bad dream. His mammy had aged violently overnight. I saw her once in the supermarket, pushing a squeaky trolley with only a single lemon rolling around in it.

The last time I ever saw him, standing at the edge of the football pitch after the bell had rung, his black hair was wet from the rain, and droplets dripped onto his face. He was shivering. His shirt was soaked, and patches of pink skin showed through. You'll catch your death, I thought, feeling suddenly, inexplicably sad. His eyes were blue, so blue, and his hair was wet from the rain.

*

One Sunday night, a few weeks after, I was curled up on the sofa after my bath when the phone rang. Mammy answered and silently mouthed to me, 'Izzy?' I shook my head. 'Oh, sorry love, she's just popped out for a while. I'll get her to call you back when she gets home,' she said, putting the phone down. 'Aoife, you know you can talk to us about anything,' she said. 'I know Mammy, but I'm fine, honest'. A dark mass spread like smoke under my chest, suffocating me.

*

I told Mammy I was going to Izzy's for a while. 'Well, don't be long,' she said. 'And take a coat.' I zipped up my parka and walked to the lake. The place was deserted, the only noise the buzzing from the dragonflies hovering at the river's edge. The lake was my favourite place. In summer, we'd go swimming in our bra and pants, as the boys would peep from behind the bushes, Patrick too, sometimes. I stripped off my jeans and t-shirt and waded into the water. It was cold and clear. I submerged my head under the water, as plops of rain started to fall, a low grumble in the distance. I swam back to shore and sat trembling on the muddy banks, knees tucked under my chin. There was a loud clap of thunder. I gripped my arms around my legs, and thought about Patrick, how he'd looked at me that day in the gym hall. About how it made me feel inside.

*

When I got back, the house was silent. I sneaked up to my room and peeled off my wet clothes, then lay on my bed in my underwear. It felt like a brick was jammed inside my rib cage. I covered my face with a pillow so nobody could hear me weep in the darkness. I hoped someone was standing over him, guarding him, screaming, screaming for all of us who couldn't.

Zain Rishi
PILLARS

Among the trees, there is a tree, the leaves
of which do not fall and is like a Muslim.
—Sahih al-Bukhari

I. Sajjada
It was as if blessing the floor below her knees was
the only way she could ever stand again. Her scarf,
black and billowing, moulded to her like a dark
calcification as she said the words, سبحان الله, and I
couldn't help saying them too. I didn't know what
they meant, only that somewhere in the rhythm of
each syllable, the roughness of the middle *h*, was
a kind of safety: something that resembled a home.

II. Taeam
Home was an unfaltering reminder that our lives
were burdened with temporality. Plastic chairs.
Plastic plates. Plastic food containers stacked like
glassy, wordless bookshelves behind the fridge.
We lived as though we were bound to leave, and
yet we could not deny our permanence, how we
pulsed out of the foreign ground like a weed, how
we only grew twofold, only deepened our roots.

III. Hadiiqa
Roots veining below my feet, I climbed higher and
higher towards the canopy. I found my Allah in the
furrows running up the tree, in the bugs that left
them just to live below my nails. I climbed higher
and higher, leaves cleaving to me like a new flesh,
dew mottling my hair as I broke out into the daylight,
forgetting, if only for a moment, the splinters in my
palms, the bark breaching my new, ascended skin.

iv. Wajah

Skin that was never scarred or spotty, only plain as
bleached canvas, only warm blood bristling under
rosy white cheeks. It meant something in me was
wrong, something I could never reach, a place
I could never inhabit, a beauty I could never keep.
Because to keep a thing was to love it, and to love
a thing was to become it. So I would put on my
own skin, every day, thinking it wasn't mine

v. Rouhi

until I knew it was hers. And there are many things
I know now. That the Devil is the name we gave to
the human condition. That there are a thousand ways
to love another boy. That I never uttered an honest
prayer, not until I knew this skin was ours, that we
grew out of foreign ground, that we fell from the
canopy, our bodies glowing with sin, and prayed
for a faith where we didn't need words at all.

SKUNKS IN THE MALL

I'm writing this down before I forget it: The dream
wasn't much of a dream. We made a ruin
of ourselves in the popcorn aisle, not questioning
why anyone would sell this many brands
of popcorn, nor why Baloo the Bear was with us
the whole time, watching. A gap in the shelves
took us to your gaff, or mine, or something
in-between where Bill Clinton spoke in bagpipe
bleats instead of words. And that bit
isn't even silly compared to the water slide
interlude that took us to the mall, which I remember
because we never call them malls. You were
so happy to be here. You told me
you wanted to stay. Of course, we didn't make it
that far. The reality
somehow escapes me. But back then, I saw it
for what it was. Us, running full pelt
across the linoleum, past those giant skunks
who joined our haste. Us, hobbit-holing out
into the amber daylight, where your hand
was the tree I'd been holding all along, a totem
of life that never made sense. You never made sense
to me, really, until then.

Romi Sarfaty
NOT SO HARD TO IMAGINE

> In the end, I have nothing new to say. Why detain you with these worn-out stories? Why this wasted time? Why archive this? Why these investments in paper, in ink, in characters? Why mobilize so much space and so much work, so much typographical composition? Does this merit printing? Aren't these stories to be had everywhere?
>
> —*Julieta Singh*

I have never been to the battlefield, just next to it. I resisted enlisting for two years. I was under surveillance by the recruitment police. In the investigation, I said that every time I hear a motorcycle, I peed myself because I'm sure it's an alarm, and they didn't believe me. They prescribed me tonnes of meds, but my parents told me not to take them because I would become numb to the bloodbath, or even worse, feel spontaneously courageous enough to bathe in it, like a jacuzzi, get there while it's hot and comforting. So I kept acting like the meds didn't work. But the truth is that I am just a coward, I was afraid to do something I don't understand. I was afraid to shoot someone out of panic.

I am armed. Too cynical and condescending to fall into some kind of delusion, to believe that something is real. I am too scared to realise that all of this is happening. Sometimes I imagine that I collected the body pieces of these best friends I had. How I idolised these friendships after they died.

I'm so scared by what people have to say, I watch to escape, I watch too much, I tell people stories of others like they're mine without noticing, **AND I WATCH THEIR MOUTHS FILL UP WITH SALIVA FROM THE HORROR**. I don't blame them, it's all so sad and anonymous. I'm so scared of what people have to say, I don't want to hear another story. I am spending my life looking at the news and waiting to see that someone I know died. Maybe it'll take the burden off my back.

List of scenes from movies that live in my brain:

No. 1 – The gang-bang scene from *Requiem for a Dream*. When Jennifer Connelly and another girl are on all fours on a white sheet, connected by a huge black dildo between their asses, and tonnes of men are cheering around them.

No. 2 – The end scene from *The Strangers*. When the main character is on her deathbed, and her husband is already dead next to her. She asks the killers why they tortured them, and they answer, 'Because you were home.'

> True the saying: 'Tis impossible to live with the baggage, impossible to live without 'em.
> —Lysistrata, Aristophanes

I wrote a new song for peace:

> We would never remember how we had dived into a deep sleep,
> and then suddenly it looks like morning again.
> It is not really the anaesthetic sleep that we're afraid of,
> but the idea that waking up proposes.
> The start-again.
> The feeling of opportunities when we have no clue.
> They start again.
> We have this feeling that we're missing the purpose,
> like we're wasting our lives,
> but we don't know what to do differently.

A little love won't hurt.
Maybe we can love each other!

Upstairs they are too busy arguing for credit,
WE ARE READY TO GIVE UP THE CREDIT,
we are tired, and we don't understand.

A little love won't hurt.
Maybe we can love each other!

No. 3 – The scene in *Gummo*, when they abuse a dead cat, hitting it like a piñata.
No. 4 – The scene in *The Pianist*, when they throw a wheelchair with a person on it out of the balcony.

I have fantasies of running away. I jump out of the window, land straight on my feet, and the overwhelming smell of the sewer in the street makes me restless. I run fast before the fear will catch me, and with every step, I break away from the dangerous human-adult I've become.

The speed smears the landscape into channels of light, I run until the cold air takes over my muscles, and only when I fall onto the ground, I realise it's no longer concrete. I spread and splash in the new soft-sticky texture, grab it in my arms, and anoint my body in it. I scream and grab my hair with my sharp dirty nails, and I pluck it all out. It doesn't ache, but I feel the burning fresh flesh of my scalp, and I don't stop to think if it's blood or tears that are running down my cheeks, because by this point I had already freed myself from the skin,
   I AM JUST MOTION.
I dig into the tender-muggy dirt, and I hear a voice calling me from the pit. I trench like a worm, following this voice and slowly the space narrows down. The rims of the space breathe in and out, press on my chest with every inhalation, and remind me I'm trapped in my pathetic selfhood. *I ask the voice:* 'what are you doing here, Mommy?' She answers that she's tired of fearing and has decided to bury herself alive, it's safer underground anyway.

She clings me to her chest, suffocates me with her love. I'm too afraid to confess that I am sad she made me human, but she knows because she feels the same. We lie there, hugging, both naked and glad that the darkness prevails us from our form.

We can hear heavy steps and hysteria from above us. Someone died, and everyone is taking pictures. My mother presses her palm on my eyes, forcing them to stay closed. I can feel her lips close to my ears and she whispers: 'Don't open your eyes, we can stay here and we'll both wear our favourite childhood dress forever. The one that has stains of runny nose and chocolate, from when we were still allowed to show that we're actually disgusting.'

> I spent too long loathing various parts of my body,
> it held me back from doing.
> —Penny Goring

I wrote once in a love spell: 'You know you can tuck your two figures in this hole and stretch my body. I am rubber and you change me to the formation you need. I will let you and would never let the army.'

> Punctuation is irrelevant to me, I just want to be understood.
> —Penny Goring

> I have to resurrect myself every new morning.
> —Penny Goring

If you divide equally the amount of ground space on Earth by the number of humans, each will get 1.65942801 metres for themselves. It is just about the average height of a human being. It means that if we all lie on the ground in a foetus position, we leave a little bit of space between us and we cover all the ground almost perfectly.

But it also means that if we each take space for ourselves, not bothering to share from time to time, there is no space left.
At all.
For no other being.
at all.
For nothing else to exist,
at all.
For no views to see,
At all.

However, if we minus the space that we all take together from the ground space on Earth, there are still 202 million square metres, for all the other beautiful things.

I see two radical possible options.

It is either we all hug. *We stand close to one another, skin touching skin, sharing one space,* **MAYBE ON THE TOP OF A BIG CLIFF, WHERE WE CAN WATCH TOGETHER EVERYTHING WE'VE BEEN SO LUCKY TO BE A PART OF.** *Maybe we can even arrange ourselves according to height so we can all observe all that is happening together. We can even walk together like a giant blob, that hovers gently around to appreciate.*

OR,

WE CEASE HUMANITY.

WE STAND ON THAT CLIFF AND PUSH ONE ANOTHER UNTIL THERE'S ENOUGH SPACE. A MOUNTAIN OF DEAD BODIES WILL COVER THE LANDSCAPE AND THE BLOOD WILL COVER THE MEMORY. WE WILL EXIT THE WORLD AND ENTER THE IMAGINARY-DELUSION-REALITY WHERE THERE IS NOT ENOUGH SPACE FOR EVERYONE TO LIE IN A COMFORTABLE FOETUS POSITION INSIDE THE HUGE BELLY OF MOTHER EARTH.

I also see one less radical option – we just shhhhhhhhhhh shhh-hhhhhhhhhh shhh shhhh shhhhhhhhhhhhh share.

Where do all the happy stories go to?

> Violence can destroy power; it is utterly incapable of creating it.
> —Hannah Arendt

No. 5 – The scene in *Pulp Fiction*, when the cop is raping the big guy.
No. 6 – The scene in *Ken Park*, when Ken shoots himself.
No. 7 – The scene in *Dancer in the Dark*, where the mom got into so much trouble just because she tried to gather money for surgery so her son wouldn't become blind like her, and she is executed and sings one last song before she dies.

'Do you want to go to the park today? I feel like running.'

'Yeah, running while screaming: the ground belongs to no one, but we tease it until it'll drop from under our feet.'

'Hahaha yeah, running and screaming: make us ground, so we'll have a living experience of how it feels to be stepped on and ignored.'

'Hahaha yeah, running and screaming: **the ground doesn't need words for mediation because it is It.**'

'Hahaha yeah, running and screaming: help! we came from the ground, and yet somehow we got lost in its dust.'

'Hahaha yeah, running and screaming: make my body your manure.'

'Hahaha yeah, running and screaming: I'm afraid we fell into the pit.'

'Hahaha yeah, running and screaming: I'm afraid we sunk in the mud.'

No. 8 – The scene in *Men*, when the main character's boyfriend commits suicide, and his body falls on the metal fence and is impaled on the spiky edges.

During my last spring at home, before I moved to Glasgow, I spent a weekend with my dad. He made us a big festive dinner and remembered that I don't like red wine, so he bought a bottle of white for me, and a red for himself. A litter of wine each to wash the bitter taste of parting, down the throat. After we ate all the food he made us, which tasted good but looked *rushed, temporary and improvised*, just like the rest of his apartment, we sat down on the outdoor sofa, in his tiny yard, and played Backgammon for hours. We were drunk and giggly, but my father insisted on acting like he wasn't. He wanted to keep his parental persona, which was hard to maintain in his hippy apartment. He kept winning the game, and around three in the morning he was in such a good mood that he was ready to throw some depressing confessions, filtered with dark humour and confusing smiles.

He said so many scattered things that I can't even remember, but around five in the morning, he covered all topics from abusive love affairs to his lack of money, to war. He was still a little influenced by the wine's fumes that embellished his courageous honesty, and as he won one last game, he finished with a victory statement: 'I feel plucked by this world'.

In the beginning, I was confused by the grinning smile that still accompanied his face, but later I realised it was his way of showing that he had no idea what to do about it. He fully stripped off his parental persona by this point, *and all I could see was a creased boy, that got beaten by . . . the game?*

When he drove me back to my mom's flat the day after, he said he'd take me through a longer way *to show me something beautiful.* We kept driving and the landscape changed slowly to these majestic golden dunes, the air was dry and warm, and my father opened the window to let the sand tickle us, so we could feel the landscape on our skin.

Suddenly he turned the car, and the texture of the dunes changed into two white mighty stones. 'We are inside the mountain's belly,' my father said. He stopped the car, and we went outside to stand between these massive rims.

IF THE MOUNTAIN HAD COLLAPSED ON US AT THAT MOMENT, I WOULDN'T HAVE CARED. I looked at my plucked dad, and his eyes sparked from the emptiness.

Inside a stone, you can find a shelter of Nothing at All.

We stretched the moment as much as we could, but the mountain didn't collapse on us, so we had to keep driving. When the city's structure began to emerge from the distance my father said: 'Some things life cannot overcome, things that go with nature, not against it. Things that surrender to change, surrender so much you can't even notice they are changing.'

It doesn't have to be a violent story, but perhaps a generous one. I choose to remember the giggles, the warm food, the warm wind, the warm sand on my face. I choose to be grateful for the mountain that let us in, or for my heartful dad who was generous with his emotions. The violence here is so hidden and subconscious that it exists almost as a separate metaphorical memory.

A piece of plucked beef that was once a human, waiting between the rims of a mountain for the debris to save him.

No. 9 – The scene in *Spirited Away*, when Chihiro's parents become pigs, and they're being whipped because they ate too much.
No. 10 – The scene in *Trainspotting*, when they show the dead baby in the cradle.

My friend and I decided that if we ever go back to academia, it is to do a PhD on the relationship between anal penetration and the reduction of violence. In other words, we believe that if once a month, every man would legally have a finger up his ass for pleasure purposes, without having to deal with any social stigma the act might carry, there won't be any war.

I think about how in *Lysistrata*, women decide to refuse having sex with men in order to stop the war. Maybe one should not attempt occupation before he ever experiences the intricate intimacy of being penetrated. Maybe the unilateral experience of only penetrating is what causes this tragic blindness of this world. Maybe we fuck each other because we actually want to be fucked.

My friend once told me that abuse is more common with men because societal codes design them not to express emotion. A man hits a woman because he's feeling sad but not allowed to cry. So, he causes her pain to see the reflection of his own feelings in someone else. Silence her with fear because he feels silenced. Free himself from the pain by passing it on.

> Before now, and for quite some time, we maintained our decorum and suffered in silence whatever you men did, because you wouldn't let us make a sound.
> —Lysistrata, Aristophanes

> We see that all that is solid melts into air, all that is holy is still profaned, and we are at last compelled to face with sober senses our real condition of life, and even more, our presence in this world.
> —VestAndPage

I DON'T HAVE ANY INTERESTING TAKES; I AM JUST SAD.

I think I don't stand anymore, I hide under the blanket, waiting for someone to rape me, or rob me, or send a rocket straight onto my head. I hide under the blanket and imagine how they break the door, put a gun to my temple and ask me what's my opinion, and I pee in my pants, because I don't have any opinions anymore, I've spiralled and spiralled and discovered nothing. I don't know how to break free from all this violence, I don't have any collective imagery of kindness to elicit change. I'm left with this non-oriented love that feels like a burden, and with guilt.

I dreamed that my love proposes to me, and I cry for days. In the dream, I'm scared for the tears to stop because I know that once they'll dry, I'll have to answer No. I love him to death, but in this life delusion, I don't believe I would ever be prepared to give up and grow up.

I am sorry,
I really tried to see through the signs,
I went to the park day after day and watched the same tree.
I tried to name all the things that make the tree into a tree,
to disassemble it into its parts, so I could stop seeing it as a whole.
I thought that if I could reach something simple, I might be able to start reaching the world. But the words were finished, and I couldn't see beyond them.
I walked back home every day feeling defeated,
realising I am forever stuck in this world I can't understand.
I have got to know so many words, touched, smelled and watched so many textures.
But these don't go with what I see in the news.
I remember!
That once I felt like it was all so wonderful!
Like I am so grateful and warm.
Like I am grateful and womb.
Most days, when I'm in my home,
I still envision the outside like this,
warm womb.
But then I leave the house
and on the way to the tree
I see all these sad, red, faces.
I look at the tree, and disassemble and disassemble,
and when I can't name anymore,
I really try to imagine,
but all I can see is my sad red face, begging the world to stop.
And I realise I am forever stuck in this war I can't understand.
I would love to marry you,
I would love to marry all the beautiful things one day,

we just need to understand first how to escape this shame and guilt we're living on.

An Arabic mom and her daughter got stuck with me inside the subway.

We had a chat that was so so lovely and warm,

that was so so lovely and womb.

She had a Palestine flag wrapped around her back, and her little daughter wrapped around her neck. The daughter was fascinated by my blinging earrings and asked to touch them. I gave her my ear and when the subway finally opened, we walked together upstairs, and the mom asked where I was from. I felt like my heart was about to speed outside my body when I said, partially whispering, partially crying, partially afraid to lose her affection,

<small>I am from Israel.</small>

I was about to add I'm so sorry, but she said that before me.

'Oh darling, I'm so sorry it must be so strange for you right now.'

She hugged me while her daughter still holding my ear.

I said I'm sorry too.

I would love to marry her as well one day.

I do.

I do.

Neil Gordon Shaw
19 SEPTEMBER 2014

Wanney thi grate nites that. An me an Broon huv hud a fair fewey them in wur time. Thickez thieves, thi pairey us. Kent thi cunt since thi skewl, thi primarey – gittin oan fur fortey yeer noo. Baithey us, sex yir auld, in Miss Addisuns class. Wee ride she wuz. A mindey Broon wan time affrin her his Turkish Dellite – thi chocklit barr, ya durtay basturt! – aw shy an that. Saft wee cunt thut he wuz at thi time. Fuckin changed daze noo.

Thi call tay erms hud went oot oan thi soshulls an boays wur firin up tay thi skwair, mair an mairey thum. A wee bit bevvied maistey thum, bit no tay much, no peakin tay soon, keepin thi pooder dry, say tay speak. Till efter thi joab in hond wuz takin carey. Jis like me an ma man Broon.

Loadsey Gers taps oan show, thi Jax flyin prowd, boays geen it Goad Save thi Kween. Fuckin triumfint man. Lang tay rein ovur us. Thi nashnal fuckin anthum, withur they nashnalist arsehols like it or no. That moab wur oan thi othur sidey thi polis, chantin thir shitey wee chants an singin Flairay fuckin Scotlin. Bit naw up fur it, ye cud tel, naw efter thi gubbin they took thi nite afore. Fuckin beawtayful it wuz. Thir dreams in tatturs. Bravehert wankurs. Fuckin joke man. Evrey cunt an his dug kens Scotlin wid be totalley fuckt wiyoot Englin. Evrey cunt cept they fuckin flag shaggurs. See aw thi money thi Royals bring in fay tourism? Kis guidbiy tay thut fur sterters. Fuckin mull-yuns a yeer. Evrey cunt in Scotlin wid be oan thi fuckin broo if it wuzney fur Englin. Bit SCOTLIN SAID NAW, YA NASHNALIST SCUM.

Maistley litewaits oan thi othur sidey thi polis, ye cud see that, even if it wuz gittin derk. A fair few lassies in thir tay. An some Hamiltun Accies an aw – ney surprize they cunts wuz yes – naw fuckin Britush onywiys.

Ye cud tel thi wiy it wuz gonney go. Thi polis werney up fur it, huddin thi line bit herts no in it. Mair than a fewey thum lookin aw nervy like, shiten it affay oor boays.

Wuz baccy ten when it kickt aff propur. Thir hud bin wee skermishes like, heer an thiyr, bit thi polis wur jist aboot huddin it thegethir. A mindey this wee nashnalist daftey near us shoutin thut Scotlin wuz a coloney, an how weed jis votit tay stay thut wuy. That wuz thi kindey pish they cunts wur comin oot wi, like Scotlin wuz in fuckin Africa man. An oor boays geen it thi Zeek Heils, gallus as fuck. An Broon, ever thi fuckin comeedgin, shoutin 'Freedum! Freedum ya pricks!' – like fay Bravehert, rippin thi pish oot thi cunts.

An then, suddunley like, thi boays in frontey us wur thru thi polis line, an we wur aw pilin thru this big gap, like a big fuckin dam breakin man, an we wur at thi cunts, an thuts when thi fun rilly stertit.

Thi nashnalists shat it prettey much fay thi aff. Thiyr tankin oot thi skwair, panickin like, evrey cunt fur thumsels, lassies screamin. An weer aw harin efter thum, shoutin we ur thi peepel, we ur thi fuckin peepel. An Broon doons wanney thum an me an hawfey duzzin boays ur oan um, like lions gittin torn intay a fuckin gazell, bootin fuck oot thi cunt. An then wur movin aggin, an thirs a car wi yes stickurs wi aw its windays in, an an auldur guy sittin oan thi groon, blud spurtin oot his mooth, an a loaday of thi yes cunts fuckin fleein aheadey us.

An a tel ye man. Thi feelin. Fuckin amazin it wuz. Pure rush, pure fuckin freedum, like ye wur ten foot fuckin tawl, indistructibel like. Ney feelin like it – naw charley, naw whizz, naw even watchin thi Famous Glasgey Rangurs scorin thi wunner agginst thi filth. Totalley in thi fuckin moment. An aw thi daytayday pish thut kin fuckin wey ye doon – like thi fuckin credit cerd dett an that monstur leckey bill, an aw thi auldur shite – like ma so-callt stepda – lang deid noo thank fuck thi sick basturt – aw that wuz a mull-yun fuckin mile away.

An me an Broon cornur this yes cunt doon a lane aff thi skwair. Boay looks like a fuckin studint. Wee poofs goat a Bairns no Bombs badge an heez huddin a Scotlin flag. An a clok its that arsehol fay thi skwair – mistur coloney boay. Naw lookin say clevur noo thi cunt. Boays totalley shitein himsel.

'Tell ye whit,' he sais, 'Why dont ye tak ma wallut.' His huddin it oot tay Broon. 'Jist tak it an lits call it kwits.'

An Broon goze, 'Relax wee man. Calm doon. Dinney worry yersel. Wur gonney tak yer wallut aff ye anyhow. An yer phone.'

Like a sais, fuckin comeedgin thi man.

An thi wee shite kens whits comin an he sais, voice aw kwaverin an that, 'Its no me thuts your enemey.'

Which tay be fair, iz naw how it fuckin looks, izit?

'Naw muchey a fuckin bravehert ur ye ya cunt,' sais Broon. An then heez weyin in, an am weyin in, an thi wee poofs oan thi deck screamin, an then Broon boots it in thi mooth, an thi cunt goes aw kwiet.

An then wur headin back intay thi skwair, fuckin buzzin man, Broon singin 'Anothur yin bites thi dust', an wur back intay thi fray.

Joey Simons
SANT EULALIA

Laia lived in a large top-floor apartment in Barcelona with bare white walls and cold white floors. She liked to fuck on the balcony and she hated it when *giris* deseeded green peppers. Growing up, her grandmother filled her head with stories of Saint Magi, a hermit and orphan who lived in a cave, and when she was thirteen years old she emulated him by running away from the family home in the village of Alcover. Her father, Joan, found her three days later eating stolen strawberries and hiding in a half-drilled well he himself had dug as part of a failed scheme to bring life to the area by irrigating farmland from the local river basin. The days and nights he spent wandering the foothills of the Prades mountains looking for her were the worst of his life, and he was never able to forgive himself or his daughter. Not long after, he got a job as a fitter in Barcelona. There he worked on alterations to a church in the barrio of Gracia and I first met Laia in the terrace of the bar that lay directly in the shadow of its imposing stone façade, near where I lived with two ex-fish factory employees from Stornoway. Her father returned to Alcover only once, to bury a brother who had shot himself in a family dispute over the grandmother's house. After that Laia never saw him again.

She herself left at the first moment she could, fleeing the silence and the hazelnut trees and the village *festas* for the endless noise of Ibiza. For a while she worked in a bar called The Highlander, and when we were together she would sometimes smile sadly and order shots in a Scottish accent. At nineteen years old, her dark hair turned blonde, her fair skin dark, and her green eyes wide, wild and blue. She followed the usual route and began selling pills to pay for the cramped room she shared with a girl from Manchester. Laia was sharp and strong, learned English quickly, and stood out from the exhausted crowds festering under the lasers and the rotting sun. The dealers soon picked her up and she drove bikes and hid guns and slept with whoever she wanted. Like the *bandolers* who roamed Alcover three centuries earlier, she scared and fascinated the rich in equal measure, and they opened the doors of their clubs and yachts to her laugh and striding walk. For five years no one could touch her.

But then something happened that she never talked about, and which I could only read in her thin nose and hoarse voice, the split in her full bottom lip, and the big white scar that wound up her right arm like the Cami del Remei. Above all I read it in her huge white eyes. They never seemed to blink and I could never look away, even when she hid them behind gold-rimmed sunglasses or stared at the ground. She left Ibiza and returned to her village and childhood room, the *ermita* of her youth, to sleep. She handed her phone and a thousand euros in cash to her mother, gave up drugs, alcohol and cigarettes, listened to no music, read no books and spoke as little as possible. Then she started to run. At first slowly, methodically, for an hour a day, usually in the morning, and only as far as the quarry on the edge of town where day and night limestone was extracted for railway ballast. When her feet began to blister, she asked her mother to buy her a pair of running shoes. Over time she learned how to breathe and began to run up into the forest proper, following the dusty hiking trails that cut steeply through the pine trees. Soon she found herself climbing six miles along the Gloriosa river twice every day, high high up to its source, past the ruins of the ancient hydroelectric works to the freezing, clear green waters of the *Nido del Aguila* – the Eagle's Nest. There she would wash off the filth of the world and the dust and the sweat that coated her powerful legs.

We went there together once, not long before we lost touch. We had driven up to Alcover, which she'd had the sudden urge to see. It was October and the *festas* and a humid heat hung in the air late into the night as she pulled me through the crowds of young Catalans playing fairground shooting games and eating *churrerias* while fireworks popped sadly in the orange sky. I had spent a painful few months teaching teenagers in another town not unlike this one, and resented their bronzed skin, easy vigour and the way they never seemed to get drunk. Laia tried to catch the eyes of the old men who sat outside the bars, talked endlessly in three languages about her father, dragged me down alleyways and up flights of stone steps, laughing and crying and drinking while I tried to keep up and work out what I found so depressing about the place and why I had agreed to come. In the end we fell asleep entangled in the back seat of her car.

The next morning I asked her to take us back to Barcelona. Laia was no longer clean by then and I offered to pay for petrol money in pills I'd bought from another English teacher at the end of the summer. Instead, we walked in silence to the Ermita del Remei where I threw up in the toilets. It was the church where her parents had been married. She told me then about her name, Eulalia, the saint crucified on a saltire, about how in the last years of Franco it still was illegal to give your child a Catalan name, and it was then I realised I had no idea how old she was. We began to walk and walk and she told me about her hermitage and her penance, the well, and all the things she couldn't say. I said I wanted to see her run, and so she did. I could only keep pace for a minute and sat down in the shade of a chestnut tree while Laia kept going until I could no longer see her.

Zusana Storrier
RENOVATIONS

renovations one
the shrinking story of the press at 58 denby street

The press in the front room of 58 Denby Street had a heavy, four-panelled door. Behind this, the cupboard's stout shelves could hold many items, though they rarely did. This was because the family who lived for eleven decades in the terraced house hadn't so many things; just darning eggs and liniments, fondness and lots of themselves. But looking at the press – with its impressive door and the knob which six generations of women named Margaret or Elizabeth polished to a round, gilded mirror – made each family member feel, just for a moment, a little like a lord.

In 1981, a woman called Julie inexpertly unscrewed the door off the press, then dragged it to a shed, which had been built three months previously in the cramped back garden. Her husband, Howard, meant to make a workbench of the old door but never did. On the cupboard's freshly painted shelves, Julie arranged, with much painstakingness, the matrimonial collection of nearly three hundred cassettes and long-playing records. The couple's two children were forbidden to go near the doorless press, but whenever both their parents were in the kitchen, they would fondle the music. The breadth, and the quality, of the recordings arrayed often made Julie and Howard feel like little lords.

In 2023, 58 Denby Street was bought by Aaron, a briefly married hospital worker with a side-line in do-ups. Guided by advice on his mobile phone, Aaron knocked out the shelves, prised off the fascia and burnt the clogged wood in the garden, the garden he'd go on to drown in dun-coloured gravel. The press was now a niche which held nothing but space. Like the rest of the walls, he painted the niche November grey. This would make the room look bigger and calmer, the internet had said. He trusted the internet, and that the house would sell. When it did, but for not as much as he'd hoped (and curiously, to another divorcee, this one called Mark), Aaron looked on the bright side and tried very hard to feel like some sort of lord, no matter how tiny.

renovations two
telling

When the work of renovating the bungalow was almost done, they put a photograph of Mrs Mackinnon – a real one they found in the house, not a print-out – in a brass frame and hung the picture in the porch. No-one commented on it. Perhaps any visitors assumed it was a relative. Alfy occasionally suggested that they write out a card for underneath the picture, with *Catherine Mackinnon, who lived in this house and worked in the bank (when there was a bank)*, but Leora said no. She didn't like having their benefactress, in the form of an annotated four-by-six snap, reduced to a museum exhibit. Also, it was verging on the sentimental and neither Leora nor Alfy were gushy types. And probably it had a fair bit to do with the overpowering effect of Mrs Mackinnon. 'We're very grateful that someone who was essentially a stranger gifted us her home,' Leora would say, while Alfy tried not to listen to this again. 'Most of our conversation was about bank transfers, but obviously that meant something to her. That's widows, you see. But at the end of the day, life belongs to the living and it's not like she had anyone else to leave her things to. We've put up a picture of her; we really don't have to prompt people to ask about the woman every time they come round.'

'We've put up a photo of you,' Leora would say next, turning from her partner, and shouting slightly, to a space next to the bin, or under the sofa, sometimes into a drawer. 'Do you hear me?'

Kirsty Strang-Roy
PERSEPHONE

He's mulching again.

Back turned to the expanse, stirring bitumen-thick barrels of bone shards and rot. He nets them down with mycelium threads that crawl from his sleeve as he nods a faint smile and waves. I wave back, where I stand, phantom pomegranate in hand.

We had the fight again last night. The one where he tries to keep me here and I remind him that I'll soon be gone. Or half gone. I'm only ever half here. I can only ever be his half-wife; wife for half the year.

I could watch him for hours, perplexed by the care that he shows the dying undergrowth surrounding our home. It's how we spend our days. He coppices and cultivates; braids dried out vines and grasses to trellises that bloom with ashen lichen. I watch as he goes about this breaking down of organic things. He takes joy in the decomposition of life into something that, he believes, might just grow again.

He mulches for me. It's a way to make rhythm; to quicken the dragging time of the underworld into something that feels more seasonal. He's trying, at least, to make it a little more tolerable.

The saddest thing about all this, is that these tiny acts of care are so often eclipsed by the horror of the job that needs done. The snipping of threads. The turning the world to snow. The turning, ever turning, of life into death. He is the one despised by so many but, really, he's the one we'll all need in the end.

I didn't choose this life. I barely remember what it was like before. Only that, one minute, I was walking among flowers, enchanted by the way they nod their heads in the breeze, not thinking they last but a flash. Not once did I think about the great unending cycle of it all.

And now I'm here. Where all there is, is all there was; a dizzying expanse of time that keeps us here. Down here. The nether, where rock runs like rivers. When you live in a forgotten place, a buried place, time ceases to matter. Rock moves and runs and melts; it courses and carves and cuts the world into layers that shift beneath your feet until you almost forget what it's like to live up above, where the flowers grow.

He steps back, admires his handiwork, and mutters something about needing a new pit. He'll dig it tomorrow. What shall we do now? he asks. He can barely look at me as we both feel the first prickle of spring somewhere above.

There will be light. A chaos of light that bounces above the rock and grabs through cracks in the shifting soil. Spring is coming. Rivers of rock can't hold me back and I'll choke through tubers and roots if I have to.

I move my foot to hide a sapling shoot that curls among the rot.

Laura Tansley
ONCE A MAN SAID TO ME FUCK YOU DAVID CAMERON

Once a man said to me fuck you David Cameron because I'm English and when I talk you can tell and also because when he asked my friend and I if we wanted a drink I said no thank you. I watched him closely afterwards, which he didn't like, and so he asked what's your problem, you know what you're really socially awkward, and I am and so I said I'm sorry because I am but I also didn't want him to talk to me again and he didn't so I guess we all got what we wanted – him an apology, me an opportunity to reflect when I'm lying on that tiny bed getting a smear test, thinking how a speculum is the size and shape of no part of me, and that nothing I eat makes me feel any better about any of this. Since then and especially when walking with my children I have started confessing to crows because I've read that corvids can remember. Today I talked to the crow that was pecking the eyes of a dead rat in Kelvingrove Park, in between the beautiful dull beats of beak on bone, about how when I die wouldn't it be fine to be laid out like that so the birds can take what they need. But with the weight of all the stupid shit I've ever said and done returned in memoriam it will take a murder to lift me. But at least that heft will make me seem important, like the way murdered bodies look on the telly when they're zipped into black bags and lugged on trolleys. When my grandma lived alone after her husbands took their lives she'd throw her leftovers out on to her lawn and clap her hands three times. This was the signal for the birds to come and have their fill and come they would fluttering on to the walls around and she would watch, swirling Palmolive into her peeling palms, offering the creatures that she knew only god loved the rind from her meat that anyone that knew her cooking would gladly have eaten given half the chance. If she clapped her hands now I'd come. But I tell the crows that if my grandma and I met now, she wouldn't like me.

That the extra note I put in the songs I sing is unnecessary but it flows out of me anyway. Once a man said to me 'Time is a point is a point is a point at which we have always already arrived at and there is no such things as tunnels just long entrances, or are they exits, do you understand?' The train of thought shared with me from across the swings in Hayburn Park. He craned for eye contact till I conceded and lost sight of my child for endless worthless seconds because I couldn't dismiss him. I lost sight of my child again glancing up at a crowd of corvids who were flapping in the evergreen trees, on top of the green fence around the basketball court, on the lampposts and the red roofs of the nice-looking houses of Hyndland. They were chattering hysterically, the racket bouncing off the buildings and around the square and I wondered if they were warning me. A sudden movement on the ground: a ginger cat with a magpie in its mouth darted between the bars of a garden gate and under a parked car. Out of the dark, the bird is let free momentarily, hobbling into the road. The bird-crowd screams before the cat tilts its head sideways and snatches, and disappears with the bird again into a different garden. We have all lost sight of the turmoil now but continue to yell. The man yells across to me, 'crows!' I make a snap of jaws with fingers and thumb and shout, 'a cat has killed one and now they're crying,' although I know the bird is almost certainly not dead yet, but I want to have been the only one to have witnessed it. The man is perplexed and moves away. I turn back to my child, see the frost steaming from the wooden climbing frames in the low sun, see that he is suddenly a football pitch away, a green bud of coat amongst the deciduous trees. Behind me a crow is pecking at a packet of rice crackers left in the pouch of our pram. The man whispers to his boy, points.

Tim Turnbull
GERALD FORD

When the cops arrive, it's in
shades and a 1960s Oldsmobile
convertible with a life-size
fibreglass Gerald Ford
in the back seat, not quite
what you'd expect in Bathgate,
but they say this Grassy Knoll
aesthetic plays nicely with a
conspiratorially inclined
populace and it puts the wind up
the local ne'er-do-wells. From
a distance, if you squint,
they look pretty cool, though
we all know cool's a busted
flush in this post-post-post-
ironic milieu, but the
fractious ginger scallywag
seen recently kicking a toddler
in the McDonalds queue has
absconded leaving family
members to start work on
his scarcely credible mitigations;
and our manager has locked
himself in his office and he's
shouting under the door that
he has lost the key and so it's
my job to sort it all out
which freight of burdensome
duty even Atlas mightn't have
shrugged off.

So the coppers say,
hop in the back with Gerald
there – whose witless plastic grin
looks uncannily like the real thing –
and let's cruise West Lothian's
pale pink gloaming until
the miscreant shows his pasty puss
again, or a New Jerusalem is built
and all are free and all flourish,
whichever comes first.

Emily Utter
SLIVERS

Mum says that after so many years, all the family dogs blend together to become the same dog.

I know what she means because when we talk about Grandma, I always say that when she ate her dinner – trying, as usual, to tell a story at the same time – her false teeth fell down as she chewed. For her, storytelling was like winding a thread around the tip of a finger: keep going until it's blue.

My brother says that when Grandma came for dinner, she always had a peach schnapps. I know that can't be true because by the time I was finishing high school that bottle in the cabinet was mostly water.

The dogs roamed the orchards and caught, then ate, barn mice. They curled up next to the fire in the evening (most nights in Mum's memory are winter ones) and blew farts so thick you could chew on them.

I always wondered how the dogs ate mice – skin, hair, and skeleton – yet somehow the only discomfort it caused them was gas.

Dad wasn't the sort to claim he walked to school uphill – there and back – in the snow but it was sacrilege to leave the house without your gloves on. If you waited out at the end of the drive way for the bus with bare hands, they'd shrink in the sub-zero temperatures and you'd end up, like my cousin Steve, with fingers frozen in time, as stubs.

The dogs, being setters, had an assortment of veterinary emergencies. The lawnmower once kicked up a stone so hard it burst the fluid sack in their front ankle joint.

Another time, the dogs stopped eating and when the vet opened them up they found a chunk of asphalt and a peach pit. After Mum and Dad spent three thousand dollars, they told the dogs *if you do this again, it's the glue factory*. We put a lid on the compost and Dad stopped hosing off the barbeque at the end of the driveway.

I'm always careful eating fish because Dad told me he once swallowed a salmon bone sideways and it got stuck in his throat that way.

At school, one of the girls in my class said you had to tie your hair back or else, in a strong wind, you could get a hair in your eye that would slice your eyeball in half. Rumour had it a girl in the year above us sucked on her hair so often that she ended up with a hairball the size of a peach in her stomach.

For me, most nights on the farm are summer ones. I'd fall asleep listening to the sound of the coyotes circling a rabbit – hooting, hysterical – half-terrified, half-thrilled by the prospect of them somehow getting inside the house.

Except when it was Christmas and the snow was so deep it touched the eave troughs, when we'd 'trim the tree' at my uncle's house. All the kids would pile into the small attic that barely had a floor and wait for a visit from Charlie the Ghost (the farmer who lived in the house before) and by the end of the night, after several wild and dramatic retellings to various aunts and uncles – and Grandma, who feigned shock better than any of them – about transparent heads and glimmers in the dark, I actually believed we had seen him.

The dogs were reluctant babysitters. They sat on my brother to keep him in line and they watched me as a baby with one eye open (because I once stuck my finger up their nose and they, according to Mum, were never the same again). When Mum had her hysterectomy, they pasted themselves up against the back of her legs while she recovered in bed.

They drooled a tremendous amount and Dad said, years before I was born, that there was no way he was going to get a big slobbery dopey-looking dog like the ones Mum had grown up with.

The dogs got out one night and roamed off our land, across neighbouring farms. The pound found them and brought them home again, but they were changed.

At some point – and I cannot say exactly when it happened – so were we.

The dogs did not survive the move. Though it was more likely cancer, we told ourselves they just couldn't acclimate to a fenced-in back yard.

Twenty years on, the farm bookends the night. Before sleep, I walk myself through the rooms of the house to be sure I remember. Then I dream about it, and when I do, either the fifty-four acres of what used to be vineyards and strawberries, apples and pears, looks like the Athabasca Oil Sands – bruised, ploughed out, and weeping – or, the sun is so strong that I see only parts of buildings, half-vistas, reflections in windows. Fanned tails scarper just out of view, around corners, into the backseats of black cars I don't recognise.

In both cases I wake grateful to have been granted a visit to that place.

We only tell stories about the farm when we're all together. I read out a memory I've written – half imagined, the only way I know how – and Mum will tell me it didn't happen that way. My brother will insist that's not how he remembers it.

The dogs, at our feet, will nod along. For they were in the habit of taking a groundhog swimming in the pond before snapping its neck, diving headlong into the pool after Dad on a scorching July afternoon. They hoovered up cherry pits and got the shits for a week.

We will tell the same stories over and over again and laugh and cry and then Dad will say he only thinks about the farm when I'm home. He'll wonder aloud if all this remembering is good for me.

When I was six, I walked out on the pond when it was only half frozen-over, even though I knew the dogs had once gone through and had to be rescued. The ice had flexed beneath me, pockets of air bubbled under the surface.

One thing we like to say is that it all happened in another lifetime.

I often wonder how it would be if we never left. If the quarry across the road had remained a quarry. If the air had been clear and fresh instead of thick with industrial ash, if black dust had not coated the inside of our windows. If we'd been able to irrigate the crops. If there was no cyanide in the water, poisoning the dogs.

Mum's winters are pristine – the snow barely walked through. My summers are hot and dry, and instead of the rumble of dump trucks carrying black sludge down our road to the landfill, there is only the bird cannon and the cicadas.

The dogs are never in my dreams about the farm. They must be someplace else, not buried beneath the iris bed, or wrapped in a blanket under the flattened vineyards, or in an urn in the cedar closet, but someplace where they are free to roam.

Mum says dogs don't mark time the same way we do. They only know that we are there with them, or we are gone.

Laura Walker
INCH

Julia, 25. She is alone except for a chair, centre stage. It's empty. Obviously empty. She considers, but sits to the side, on the floor.

Julia It's Saturday. I meet a girl in the toilets of a club. It's the sort of club where they don't clean the toilets very well but we don't really care. She's sitting on the sinks. She doesn't realise the tap's dripping and her skirt's getting wet and I don't realise the floor is so dusty that my dress is going to be wrecked by the time I stand up. She's French. I'm drinking her in, gulping her. Her face is still fully on but her nipple is just slightly poking out of her bra. It's not weird though. She's baring her soul to me right now, a nip slip is the least of our worries.

She's telling me about how she was assaulted last year. We're friends right now. Close. And then she gets down off the sink and sits next to me. Her words are slurring a bit but her voice is like hot chocolate, warm and sweet and creamy and thick with accent. And she smells fantastic, like fucking brilliant. Her breath is delicious even though it's been soured by vodka. She slips her hand into my hair and pulls me closer to her and just when her face is what – an inch?

Julia holds up her thumb and fingers, approximating an inch.

Yeah, an inch. She's an inch away and she says, low and French, 'is this all right?' and I nod, really really nod and lean in. I see the next bit happen like it's happening to someone else. Like it's not my body doing it. Her lips are on mine but something goes wrong. The masala I choked down earlier bubbles back up. And onto her. Or more precisely – into her mouth.

But she's so brilliant – she's so cool. This girl has my sick in her mouth and rinses it out like it's nothing. She tells me it's all right, and that my lips tasted nice. And she asks me if I'm okay – and I'm not – but I tell her I'm sorry and I buy her a drink. I think about how close she was to my face and I wonder if she could have read my thoughts. And now I want to go home. The club's too loud and the pretty girl I kissed tastes of vomit and I have that feeling, that horrible fucking feeling all over my body that I'm so sick of having. And she touches my arm, because she's nice and she can see me standing like a fucking lemon in the middle of the club. But it's one step too far. One inch too close. So I go home. And I can't believe I've done it again.

It's Sunday. When I wake up I'm not thinking about her. I'm thinking about him. I stare at the ceiling and try to blink away my thoughts. Try to stop imagining this weird Franken-image of him and her. His body where hers was. Her voice coming out of his mouth. And I hate that I think it but I think it over and over again. How close did he get? How much did he see?

I could do this all day.

But I get in the shower. Don't look in the mirror. Realise I didn't brush my teeth last night and I still have that vomit taste in the back of my throat. I wish I'd gotten her number. I wish I'd gotten her name. Because I wanted her and I haven't wanted something in ages. And if I were different, I could have had her. I'd have made her toast in bed this morning. And I wouldn't have thought about the crumbs in the sheets.

I skip breakfast.

Alice texted me last night after I left. Five scissor emojis. She thinks she's so smart. I send a laughing face. I get in my car. I don't want to do this. I don't want to do this.

I start the engine.

I'm at work. I don't know how I got here. I'm scooping ice cream. The chill from the freezer is helping my hangover. But I can hear the tap in the kitchen, it's dripping and it reminds me of the French girl. I want to think about how she was careless. In the best way. She didn't care that she got wet because she knew she would dry. She didn't care that I puked in her mouth because she knew she'd get the taste out. She didn't care about the guy who slipped his condom off without telling her, it was just something she told strangers in the toilets now. But I'm not thinking about that. I'm wondering if he will ever come to this cafe. I'm wondering if I'll drive past him on my way home or bump into him in the shops.

Alice texted me back. 'How was she? Are you going to see her again?' I'll reply to her later.

I'm watching myself scoop now. From above. Vanilla. Pistachio. Cookie Crumble. My body looks wrong. It looks obscene. It's arched over, twisted and overtly sexual. It's indecent. It's inhuman. My face is hanging in a way that I hate. My wrist is awkward and my knee is flexed and my leg looks impossible. My breathing is so fucking loud. And every customer has his face. And every customer has her sweet French voice.

My phone buzzes. Alice. 'I hope you're all right.' I turn it off.

Vanilla. Triple chocolate. Vanilla again. The tap drips. I need to go home. I don't want to do this.

I hate that I still know his name. I hate that he only had to tell me it once, drunk and slurring, but it sits in my ears. Echoing around my skull. I hate that I know what he looks like. I know every crevice and line and pore and the way it all changes when he talks. And I hate that I know all of this about someone that I hate. And I don't know the French girl's name. In my head her face is just a mash of eyeliner and lipstick above a rogue nipple.

Going home. Shouldn't be driving. I'm watching that night with him over and over. Watching it from above. Watching it from an inch away. I can smell his breath, it's like sulphur, stings my skin, like cheap vodka in a papercut. I look mangled. My body is padded by baby fat and it's bruising under his fingers. My leather skirt around my waist. My cotton pants around my ankles. The bodies morph and I can't tell what's him and what's her. It's a wriggling, muffled mass. And it's all that I can see.

Home. It's late now. Still watching it. Torturing myself. I want to make it hurt more so I confront it in the mirror. Naked. Full length. But something about looking at it now, like this, eye to eye, something about it makes it human again. Because this body doesn't look like that one anymore. It doesn't look like the body he mangled. And I wonder if there's a single cell on it that remembers him. Biologically. And I think about how unforgivable it was, to take a child's body from them and teach them to hate it. And I get a wave of sadness and I don't feel my hatred anymore. Sadness for that girl.

Beat.

It's just a body.

The tap drips. And I let myself think about her properly for the first time today. Only her and truly her. Without any of it soured by the memories that have sat behind my eyes for the last ten years. I reconstruct her face in my head, her crevices, her pores, her wrinkles and freckles and lines, every beautiful fucking line. And if it were possible, I'd do it all again and hold my fucking nerve and hold my fucking stomach. And let her close to me. Feel her breath against my skin.

Julia sits on the chair.

I'd be in the club again. The French girl. This time I'd perch next to her on the sinks and my dress would get wet. I'd ask her what her name is. It's Jennette – or Claudette. It's Claudette. 'That's a beautiful name,' I'd tell her. And she'd put her hand in my hair and I'd lean in, an inch away [*shows us*], less maybe. And I wouldn't believe this next bit is happening to me. 'Is this all right?' I'd ask her, first this time. And she'd nod, like really really nod.

Lynnda Wardle
VISITING CAIRNBAAN

Is there not a paint named Argyll Greyblue
for January sun warming brown to green
that inks water below Butter Bridge,
the exactness of hills mirrored
in the water, where a lone fishing boat
lies marooned on its own reflection?

I do that walk again,
the one along the Crinan Canal
where our old cottage sits
white against the blue hill
or perhaps it's a black rock
where the red phone box you used to call me from
houses a defibrillator and book exchange.

Cairndubh Cottage has its curtains pulled
a house with its eyes shut tight.

I'm held by that window, its dark square
where I used to stand barefoot in summer
stretching like a woman in a painting, in love
with the giant Gunnera's soft
elephant ears and the blazing fireweed,
everything waterskin blue and summer flushed,
stroked alive by the wind.

Christie Williamson
AT INVERBOYNDIE

as trow da windoo
       lang lost tae da seawird gæls

           I glimpse da nawtheen
wir med fur

    an on da waa
          o da kirkless noo yaird

           I see whit's left
o a butterflee

       at's come here tae dee.
       Descanse en paz

           mi peerie jool
       an micht da winds

       at liftit de oot
           o da dark spun womb

du cam tae be desel in
       see dy laek agien

           whan da sun at's slippin
        dis laund o ston

    grips her agien
      seekin life

           whaur eence da grave
           reined supreme.

Robin Lindsay Wilson
RISK AVOIDANCE

Friends divert your anger,
with a well-poured Guinness
and a shared packet of nuts.
You're a zero hours counter,
a gig-economy first responder –
mannerly at the food bank.

There's a levelled heap of slag,
where you dream of a forest –
a row of bird shit tenements,
where you collapse and cheat
at cards and family obligations.

There's only booze and children –
an armchair for daytime television
and a false scent of infidelity,
to keep your ego functioning.

Finally, you borrow a fishing rod –
drag your teenage son to the river,
to teach deferred expectations
and how to deplete fantasy.

The idiot captures wet wipes –
snags the line on lager cans,
catches trees behind his head,
until your virtue feels like service
and he settles to his iPhone.

Down at the Louden Tavern,
he'll order what makes him sick,
and then revives his grin.

He'll tread in your footsteps
and man-hug scowling friends,
who don't know how to help.

BIOGRAPHIES

Craig Aitchison's poetry has appeared in *Poetry Scotland*, *Lallans* and *Nutmeg*. He has won the Badenoch Prize, the Wigtown Poetry Prize for Scots, the Burrell Collection's Hidden Treasures competition and a Scottish Book Trust New Writers Award. This year he will publish a long poem about the River Tweed.

Sharon Black is from Glasgow and lives in a remote valley of the Cévennes mountains in France. She has published four collections, her latest *The Last Woman Born on the Island* (Vagabond Voices, 2022) and *The Red House* (Drunk Muse, 2022). She also has a pamphlet, 'Rib' (Wayleave, 2021). **www.sharonblack.co.uk**

Niki Brennan is a writer and poet from Glasgow, based between there and Berlin. He has been published in *Gutter* and *The Rialto*, amongst others. He placed first in the Vernal Equinox prize and was shortlisted for the Bridport prize. He's working on both his first collection and first novel.

Kevin Cormack is from Kirkwall and writes character-driven poetry in the Orcadian dialect. His work has featured in various publications, including *Magma*, *Swiet Haar* and thi wurd's *Earthly Rewards*. His debut chapbook 'Toonie Void' was published by Abersee Press in 2021.

Born in Sofia and based in Edinburgh, **Mila Daskalova** is an award-winning researcher at the University of Glasgow. She writes academically about nineteenth-century literature and psychiatry and writes poetry and prose about everything else. She is currently working on her first collection of short stories.

Rodge Glass is the author of eight published books since 2005, across fiction and nonfiction. He is the winner of a Somerset

Maugham Award for Nonfiction and the Anne Brown Essay Prize. His most recent book is *Joshua in the Sky: A Blood Memoir* (Taproot, 2024).

Reyzl Grace (reyzlgrace.com / @reyzlgrace) is a Pushcart-nominated poet, translator, and librarian with work in *Lallans*, *Eemis Stane*, and other magazines, as well as an editor for Psaltery & Lyre. She lives in Minneapolis (USA) with her novelist girlfriend, arguing over which of them is the better writer. (It's her girlfriend.)

Lydia Harris has made her home in the Orkney island of Westray. Her first full collection, *Objects for Private Devotion*, published by Pindrop in 2022, was placed on the longlist for the Highland Book Prize. Her second collection, *Henrietta's Library of the Whole Wide World*, was published in 2024 by Blue Diode.

Stella Hervey Birrell is an award-winning poet whose work has been shortlisted for the Bridport award, highly commended by the Poetry Archive, and published in a range of places including *Magma* and *Acumen*. Her sell-out pamphlet was published in 2021 by Algia Press.

Award-winning author **Elisabeth Ingram Wallace** lives off-grid in the Cairngorms. She writes flash, short stories, and a novel. Highlights include: 'Corvidae' (Mogford Short Story Prize), 'Opsnizing Dad' (Kaleidoscope Writing the Future Award), a Scottish Book Trust New Writers Award, and Pushcart Prize and Ivor Novello nominations. Find her at **elisabethingramwallace.com**

Karen Jones has won first prize in the Cambridge Flash Prize, Flash 500, and Reflex Fiction. She is an editor for National Flash Fiction Day anthology. Her novellas-in-flash, *When It's Not Called Making Love* and *Burn It All Down*, are published by Ad Hoc Fiction and Arroyo Seco Press respectively.

Allie Kerper is a poet and editor based in Edinburgh. Her debut collection *Pale Hairs Reach Between Us* was published in 2021 with Blue Diode Press. Her writing has appeared in *Gutter*, *Wet Grain*, *SPAM zine* and elsewhere. She has performed at events such as Hidden Door and QueerBait Cabaret.

Writing in Gaelic, English and Polari, Edinburgh-based **Marcas Mac an Tuairneir** is Poet-in-Residence at the Balmoral Hotel and was Makar of the Federation of Writers (Scotland) 2024. Fourth collection *Polaris* was shortlisted for The Derick Thomson Prize and Saltire and Saboteur Awards, before landing a National Gaelic Award – **marcasmac.scot**

'S ann à Dùn Dèagh a tha **Donnchadh MacCàba**. Tha an obair aige air nochdadh ann an iomadh iris, le STEALL, *New Writing Scotland* agus *Poblachd nam Bàrd* nam measg, agus air a' bhloga An Deireag. Choisinn e an dàrna àite airson bàrdachd aig Mòd an Òbain 2024.

Crìsdean MacIlleBhàin's tenth collection of Gaelic poems *Beanas / Venus* will soon appear with Francis Boutle Publishers, and an eighth book of translations from the Russian of Marina Tsvetaeva *Roland's Horn: Poems 1917 to 1925* with Shearsman Books. An Italian anthology of his poems appeared in 2023 as *Non dimenticare gli angeli* and a Catalan anthology is in preparation, entitled *Diu el fang al terrissaire*.

Scott McNee's short fiction and poetry have been published in *Cosmic Horror Monthly*, *Beneath Ceaseless Skies*, *New Writing Scotland 40*, *Vastarien*, *Tether's End*, *Kalopsia*, *Gutter*, *Quotidian* and *The Grind*.

Kevin MacNeil is from the Outer Hebrides. He is a widely published and broadcast novelist, poet, short story writer, and dramatist.

His books include *Inner Hearts, Outer Hebrides* (forthcoming), *The Brilliant & Forever*, and *Love and Zen in the Outer Hebrides*. He edited the two-volume collected English stories of Iain Crichton Smith, as well as *Robert Louis Stevenson: An Anthology*, selected by Jorge Luis Borges and Adolfo Bioy Casares.

Kathleen J. Marshall was speechwriter to First Minister Alex Salmond. She wrote 'The Sum of His Misfortunes' as part of her PhD at Edinburgh University, and is now seeking literary representation. The novel explores masculinity in crisis, and questions the cultural trope of the Scottish hard man.

Philip Miller lives and works in Edinburgh. He is the author of *The Blue Horse* (2015), *All The Galaxies* (2017), *The Goldenacre* (2022), *The Hollow Tree* (2024) and *The Diary of Lies* (2025). His poetry has been published online and in print. His collection *Blame Yourself* was published in 2024 by Nine Pens.

Victoria NicIomhair is a bilingual poet writing in English and Gaelic, based in the Highlands of Scotland. Inspired by her family and the landscape of her home, her poetry explores themes of memory, heritage, and place. Her work has been featured in various anthologies celebrating contemporary Scottish voices.

Audrey Niven is a Scottish writer and creative coach based in London. Her stories are widely anthologised and have been nominated for Pushcart and Best of the Net awards. She is also the Founder and Editor in Charge at The Propelling Pencil short fiction journal and charity flash competition.

Amy Jo Philip is the first out transgender priest in the Scottish Episcopal Church. Before transitioning, she published two pamphlets with HappenStance and two full collections with Salt

– *The North End of the Possible* (2013) and *The Ambulance Box* (2009). She is currently working on a collection for Blue Diode.

Petra Johana Poncarová is an academic and translator. Her poems have appeared in *Aimsir* and *New Writing Scotland* 42 (under the pen name 'Johana Egermayer'). In 2025, she received a New Writers Award (Scottish Book Trust and Gaelic Books Council).

Julie Rea is an award-winning writer. She has been placed or shortlisted in many competitions, including The Bath Short Story Award and The Mslexia Short Story Competition. Her fiction is widely published in literary journals and anthologies, such as *Gutter* and *The Cormorant*. She has been nominated for The Pushcart Prize.

Zain Rishi is a writer and bookseller based in Edinburgh. He won third prize in the 2024 Oxford Poetry Prize and is a Young Poets Network prize-winner. His work has appeared in *Fourteen Poems*, *Horizon*, *Gutter* and *Propel*. He is currently working on his debut poetry pamphlet. Instagram: **@zain.rishi**

I'm **Romi Sarfaty**, and I make performance and visual art, illustrations, and I practice messy and dyslexic writing. My work is inspired by worlds of fantasy and make-belief, associative streams of consciousness, iconography and the images that emerge from acknowledging the abundance. In my practice, I work with abstraction, absurdity and melodrama, and I'm drawn to present and/or celebrated things in their most extreme, grotesque and desperate form.

Neil Gordon Shaw's memoir, *Beyond Grey*, about three years in post-communist Poland, was the Scottish Association of Writers' Non-Fiction Book of the Year. His fiction has appeared in *New Writing Scotland*, *Berfrois*, *Interpret* and the Edinburgh Anthologies Series. He lives in Edinburgh and is on X **@neil_writing**

Joey Simons is a writer and artist from Glasgow. He is the editor of *Let Us Act for Ourselves: selected works of Freddy Anderson* and, with Henry Bell, *Now's the Day, Now's the Hour: poems for John Maclean*. His commission for the Alasdair Gray Archive can be found in *Gutter* 31.

Zusana Storrier's fiction has been published in the UK and North America. She loves writing about people with hidden disadvantages who rebel against their fates. She's worked as an ethnologist, with particular interest in domestic life, so she always enjoys writing about houses and the people in them. **zusanastorrier.com**

Kirsty Strang-Roy is a writer, bookseller and facilitator living in Glasgow. Her work explores a sense of place through seasonal shifts and excavations of deep time. She teaches the Write Like a Grrrl course and creative writing workshops in collaboration with organisations such as Arkbound, The Barn, SMHAF and Glasgow Life.

Laura Tansley's visual poetry collection, *Notes to Self*, was published by Trickhouse. Her co-written collection of short stories with Micaela Maftei, *The Reach of a Root*, was published by Vagabond Voices. She lives in Glasgow.

Tim Turnbull's most recent publication is his third collection of poetry, *Avanti!* (2018), from Red Squirrel Press. A pamphlet, 'Our Lady Brings Tidings', is forthcoming from the same publisher.

Emily Utter is a Canadian writer who lives in Aberdeen. Her writing has been widely published in magazines and journals, including *Gutter*, *Northwest Review*, *Geist*, and the best of Canadian flash fiction anthology, *This Will Only Take a Minute*. She was shortlisted for the Discoveries Prize in 2023.

Laura Walker is a playwright hailing from Aberdeenshire. She began writing drama at the University of St Andrews, where she co-founded her theatre company, TPTC. TPTC are taking her third play to the Edinburgh Fringe in 2025, entitled *24 Weeks*. Her works centre most urgently Gender-Based Violence and reproductive rights.

Lynnda Wardle's work has appeared in publications including *Gutter, New Writing Scotland, thi wurd,* and *New Orleans Review*. She has participated in collectives including DeathWrites, off-page, and Writing the Asylum and is currently completing an MFA at the University of Glasgow. www.lynndawardle.com

Christie Williamson is a Shetlandic poet, essayist and translator based in Glasgow. His debut pamphlet 'Arc o Möns' won the Calum MacDonald Memorial Award. Two full-length collections of his work have been published by Luath Press – *Oo an Feddirs* (2015) and *Doors tae Newye* (2020).

Robin Lindsay Wilson is a lecturer in Acting and Performing at Queen Margaret University, Edinburgh. His work has appeared in many literary magazines including *The Amsterdam Review, Poetry Salzburg,* and *Acumen*. Cinnamon Press has published three full collections of his poetry – *Ready Made Bouquets* (2007), *Myself and Other Strangers* (2015) and *Backstage in Paradise* (2019). His poems have been awarded places and prizes in many competitions including the National Poetry Competition.